COME BY
HERE

COME BY HERE

a novella and stories

TOM NOYES

[signature]

Thanks much.
Give me a buzz @
814 806 4155

Autumn House
Press

PITTSBURGH

"Autumn House" and "Autumn House Press" are registered trademarks owned by Autumn House Press, a nonprofit corporation whose mission is the publication and promotion of poetry and other fine literature.

Autumn House Press Staff
Editor-in-Chief and Founder: Michael Simms
Co-Founder and President: Eva-Maria Simms
Managing Editor: Giuliana Certo
Assistant Editor: Christine Stroud
Fiction Editors: Sharon Dilworth, John Fried
Treasurer: J.J. Bosley, CPA
Fundraising Consultant: Anne Burnham
Community Outreach Consultant: Michael Wurster
Media Consultant: Jan Beatty
Contest Consultant: Heather Cazad
Tech Crew Chief: Michael Milberger
Intern: Chris Duerr

 Autumn House Press receives state arts funding support through a grant from the Pennsylvania Council on the Arts, a state agency funded by the Commonwealth of Pennsylvania, and the National Endowment for the Arts, a federal agency.

ISBN: 978-1-932870-93-0
Library of Congress Control Number: 2013950239

FOR A.J., JOSIE AND WYATT

With special thanks to my friends and colleagues at Penn State Erie, The Behrend College, especially Eugene Cross, George Looney, Gayle Morris, Greg Morris, Aimee Pogson, Joshua Shaw, Kim Todd and Craig Warren

And gratitude to the following organizations for their support: Penn State Behrend's School of Humanities and Social Sciences, Penn State University's Institute of Arts and Humanities, Pennsylvania's Council on the Arts, and The Sustainability Arts Foundation

And appreciation for the fine publications in which earlier versions of some of these stories first appeared: *Ascent, Barn-Owl Review, Image, New Ohio Review, Sycamore Review* and *Terrain.org*

CONTENTS

SOUL PATCH

Fresno, Fargo, Toledo. Albany, Tallahassee, Boise. When my crew and I crash a wedding—we time it so I'm rushing the aisle just as the bride and groom lean in for their kiss—the church erupts in confused gasps and worried whispers. Oliver, my best friend and agent, himself a three-time groom, holds the opinion that, in terms of nerves and anxiety, weddings are worse than funerals. With a funeral, what's done is done. With a wedding, futures are at stake. O.'s theory could explain why things get hairy sometimes for the show and me.

Three seasons ago in Dallas, the bride's stepfather, an ATF agent, stood and drew his service revolver just as I reached the altar. And then there was last season at the synagogue in Baltimore, where one of the groomsmen, a former D-1 linebacker, squared me up, yarmulke to sternum, knocking me flat and breathless. Eventually, though, the spectators, ushers, bridesmaids and clergy recognize me, and relief sets in, and then euphoria. Kingsley Carter and his show *New Digs for Newlyweds* are in the house, and it's all good.

Happiness can be just as overwhelming as distress, though, and we've had more than a few brides faint as a result of our arrival. I won't lie: a fainting bride is a beautiful thing, as sweet and tender as the baby's breath in her bouquet, and, fortunately, we've never once had one hit the deck. They're always caught, if not by their beloved, then by yours truly. We had a groom go down in season five, though, and that was a different story. No one got to him in time—no one, including myself, even made an attempt—but he ended up being OK. His collapse was slow and gradual, like he'd been hit with a tranquilizer dart. The ring bearer, the groom's nephew, was the first responder. He knelt and eased his velvet pillow under his uncle's dizzy head. Sweet kid. Cute as they come in his little bow tie, his little cummerbund, his little mop-top haircut. I'm not used to being upstaged, but I'll admit this kid stole the scene, the whole episode. Our audience lapped him up. I'm the first to admit reality TV has its limitations, but there's no denying that sometimes it's hard to beat.

After the ceremony, at the reception, the crew and I make the rounds, interviewing family and friends to get a feel for the couple: what their personalities are, how they met, the highlights and lowlights of their courtship, etc. We already know the basics—the show screens nominated couples, and up until recently, I was under the impression that the process was thorough and rigorous—but at the reception we want to flesh out the details. What we're after finally are funny quotes and embarrassing but sweet anecdotes that will play well with our primetime Friday night audience.

Eventually we sit down on-camera with the couple themselves, and even though most already know the score, we explain to them the nuts and bolts for the benefit of any new viewers at home. The upshot: while the couple's away on an all-expense-paid two-week honeymoon, we build them their dream house.

Believe it or not, some couples whine off-camera about where we're sending them for their trip. They're told we're setting them up at a Caribbean island resort, and they ask, "Any chance we could get that ski trip you sent Dan and Tricia on in Season One?" Or they're told they're going on a cruise, and they come out with, "You guys ever send anyone to Disney World? 'Cause we'd be down for that." Get over yourselves, is what I think. Plus, we have no wiggle room. Destinations are up to our sponsors.

Of the three honeymoons he's had, O. maintains that his humblest was his favorite. He took his second and third wives to Paris and Barbados, respectively, but he and his first bride, Lynnette, just hunkered down for a week in a Seattle bed and breakfast, and to this day he has trouble talking about it without choking up. The two of them, O. and Lynnette, have recently reconnected—after all these years, it looks like they're going to take another hack at it—and I couldn't be happier. I was O.'s best man at his last two weddings, and both times I knew he was doomed long before the ink was dry on the marriage license. Lynnette was the only keeper of the bunch. In my business, you learn that sometimes the first take is the only one you need. There's a lesson there, a lesson some of these show couples who bellyache about their honeymoon destinations might consider.

Eventually, though, even the most headstrong brides and grooms cooperate. *New Digs for Newlyweds* has never had a full-blown mutiny over a honeymoon or anything else for that matter. Never before our most recent couple, that is. Lawrence and Donatella Jagow-Mancuso. Larry and Donna. Given my role in what went down, I have a lot riding on how things shake out. There's the possibility of legal and PR fallout, of course, but maybe even more importantly, there are questions of my future with *New Digs*, my future with O., and, relatedly, my aspirations to be an actor, a real actor, as opposed to spending the rest of my working days as a reality show host. So I'm at a crossroads. A few of them.

New Digs was drawn to Battle Creek, Michigan, and to Larry and Donna because of the Kalamazoo River oil spill. This spill didn't get nearly as much press as the much larger BP mess in the Gulf of Mexico or, going back further, the *Exxon Valdez* catastrophe off the coast of Alaska—one of the things Donna told me during our fateful night together was that people have inherently stronger feelings about oceans than they do rivers—but the environmental impact of the Kalamazoo River spill was significant. During the time we were shooting, there was some suspense building—this was good for the show—around the question of whether or not the cleanup crews were going to be able to contain the spilled oil, more than a million gallons' worth, before it reached Lake Michigan, which supplies the drinking water for more than ten million Americans. So all things considered, the Battle Creek site had the makings for some pretty good TV.

Of course, not only was there a tragic, compelling storyline unfolding, but there were lots of tragic, compelling images to go along with it, including the obligatory shots of petroleum-soaked birds, mostly ducks and herons, being washed with dish detergent by rubber-gloved volunteers. Gets me every time no matter how many times I see it. There's the bird, a totally helpless creature, who, despite its fear and lack of understanding, is having its life saved. You want to explain the whole thing to the bird. You want to apologize for the mess it's in, but then you also want to impress upon it how lucky it is to be receiving help. Of course, you can't explain any of this to the bird, and there's sadness in that communication gap, I think. That's just one level of sadness, though. The longer you let the shot work on you, the more levels there are. On top of the communication gap sadness, maybe you think of all the oil-soaked birds that aren't being helped, maybe it hits you that there are way more birds than there are volunteers. So there's that sadness. Hopeless numbers sadness. Plus, faced with the image of this selfless, rubber-gloved volunteer, maybe your conscience throbs a bit, maybe you feel some conviction about how you yourself should do more good in the world, about how you're way too self-interested. So there's that self-hating level of sadness maybe. But there's more than that even. There's the symbolic-level, psychological-level sadness. Maybe for whatever reason you start feeling yourself like an oil-soaked bird in need of a good scrubbing. It's like the shot is reminding you of how dirty you are and of all of the ways in which you're dirty. Plus, I think there's just something inherently sad about rubber gloves, especially yellow ones that stretch almost the whole way up to the elbows. And some of the volunteers wear goggles or surgeon masks over their mouths and noses, which suggests that there's danger in the air, so there's a certain level of fear conveyed in the shot, and fear is a kind of sadness.

On my laptop, I've got one of the Battle Creek dirty bird stills as my background wallpaper. It's a green heron being scrubbed clean by two college-aged kids, one guy and one girl. When I'm working on my screenplay—it's really good now, focused and tight, and I know O. would agree if I could just get him to read the damn thing with an open mind—I like knowing that the girl and the boy and the oily bird are hovering there behind my open document window. Like muses.

The show liked Larry and Donna as characters for the same reasons it liked Battle Creek as a setting. Prepackaged dramatic tension. They were what's known around the set as a gimmick couple. Two or three times a season, *New Digs* tries to work one in. Last year we built a house for a 7'1" groom and his 4'2" bride, and in Season Two we did a special needs home for a blind woman and her wheelchair-bound husband. Along the way, there's also been the Jewish-Catholic newlyweds, the Democrat-Republican newlyweds, and for our July 4th show, we built a home for two Iraq War veterans, the bride a marine and the groom army infantry. In the case of Larry and Donna, their gimmick was that he worked for BridgeCo, the oil company responsible for the oil spill, and she worked as an enforcement agent for the regulatory body, the Pipeline and Hazardous Materials Safety Administration, who was trying to put the screws to him and his cronies. Love can conquer all, right? There's an innate human desire to want to believe that, I think. Our fans always love the gimmick couple episodes. Gives them what they think they need.

Larry and Donna's relationship had been defined from the beginning by disasters, and their love had grown with each new tragedy. Their story was that they'd met in Minnesota when Larry, on behalf of BridgeCo, argued with Donna and other industry safety officials about an incident in which two pipeline workers had been killed in an explosion. Most couples start off with small talk, move onto flirting. Larry and Donna's initial conversations involved dickering back and forth about dead men. A year or so later, their paths re-crossed and their relationship progressed in northern Wisconsin, where BridgeCo spilled 200,000 gallons of crude in a wetlands area during a pipeline expansion project. Accusations and denials. Buck-passing and lawyer-speak. Plea bargains and lowball estimates. Not exactly the language of love. Or maybe I'm wrong about that. What do I know?

On more than one occasion during the night Donna and I spent together in my Motor Coach, I wanted to ask her about her history with Larry. As an actor slash aspiring screenwriter slash maybe even one day director, I try to figure out people as characters, try to identify and understand the nature of the desires and fears that make them tick. There's a thin line between passion and fear, and another one between innocence and guilt, and still another between justice and mercy, and it seemed to me that Larry and Donna had tightrope-walked all of them.

I never got around to asking Donna about her and Larry's history, though. Given the situation, I couldn't figure out how to do so without upsetting her, and I didn't want to say anything that would make her leave. I'll admit it. I liked her there with me.

While I know it was selfish of me to want her to stay, I also think it would've been wrong of me to send her away. Yes, it was her wedding night. Yes, she was confused and perhaps still slightly buzzing from the myriad champagne toasts made at the reception to honor the vows she and her groom had just taken. Yes, what happened sounds tawdry, but it wasn't only tawdry. And if it was dumb, it wasn't only dumb. There was something else, something good underneath the selfishness and tawdriness and dumbness, and I was tuned into that good thing. For better or worse.

Despite the fact that O. and I are not lately seeing eye to eye—on account of the trouble I'm in with the show because of Donna, of course, but also on account of our differing visions for the future of my career—there's no denying he's a dynamo of an agent. I've told him as much, and I'll tell him again when he simmers down, comes off his high horse, sees fit to listen instead of just preach. Yes, I'm in some trouble now, and by extension O.

is in some trouble, and I'll need to be extra careful about minding my p's and q's for a while until all this blows over, but I can't imagine that *New Digs* would decide to cut me loose. That's not me being arrogant; that's just me understanding how the business works. Without Kingsley Carter, there is no *New Digs for Newlyweds*.

After O.'s and my last phone conversation, which ended with him hanging up on me, my first instinct was to text him a reminder in the form of a question: "Who's working for who, O.?" I resisted, though, took the high road in hopes for peace, and called him back. When I got his voice-mail, I said, "This too shall pass, O.," and I told the sweet sonofabitch that I love him like a brother. "If there's no Oliver Upchurch, there's no Kingsley Carter," I told him. "To not realize this I'd have to be a fool."

Again, though, O.'s brilliance and savvy aside, when it's lights-camera-action, when the show is on-site and shooting, it's not about O., not even a little, and it's not about network executives, and it's not about sponsors, and the dirty truth is it's not even really about the newlyweds. It's all about me. It's about my waxy, tapered sideburns; my firm pecs in my tight, sleeveless work shirt; my hip-clinging tool belt; my steel-toed boots; my Nike hard hat; my Mr. Clean hoop earrings; my relaxed fit button-fly's; and my amber-tinted safety goggles. It's about what O. has referred to in the happier past as my triple money-makers—my sapphire eyes, my radiant smile and my cleft chin—and it's about what's smack-dab in the middle of these winning features, what's hovering in that liminal space that's not quite mouth, not quite chin. It's about my soul patch.

A gesture toward hipness? I suppose that's part of it. Who's not after the 18–34 demographic? Truth is, though, I had other, more substantial reasons for sprouting my patch. Beatnik jazz musicians invented the concept. The whiskers between their bottom lips and chins cushioned their faces against the mouthpieces of their horns. So it looked cool, but it also had purpose. Two sides of the same coin, and what I'm all about. My soul patch isn't just a marketing tool. It's meaningful in light of what I currently do, build high-quality, breathtaking homes on TV, and what I want to do in the not too distant future, act in movies. Not just any movies, though. Not art house films that no one but the occasional academic egghead sees or understands, but not stupid shoot 'em up blockbusters or anything starring robots or set in space either. I want to be part of pictures with heart, with integrity. Pictures that depict the human soul in conflict with itself, that speak to and evoke the healing and redemptive potential of beauty and truth. And while I know integrity can't be bought, that beauty and truth aren't for sale, I'm looking for projects with at least some potential for box office appeal, productions which, even in a small way, can help breathe life into our nation's floundering economy. Not just form, but function, too. Sign me up.

I love what I do on *New Digs*—I do—and I tell O. this. "Don't get me wrong, O.," I say. We get in these back-and-forths about my career, my future. O. thinks *New Digs* is as good as it gets. He thinks we've reached the pinnacle. He wants the show to run forever, for my current list of sponsors—jigsaws to jeans, hammers to hair gel—to write their checks forever, for my do-it-yourself home repair website to keep getting hits forever. "We've made it. We're there. Where we want to be," O. says. "Now it's just about maintenance. This is the gravy. Maintenance is the gravy." If I didn't know better, I might suspect he doesn't think I have what's required to make the transition to the big screen. If I didn't know better, I might think this.

O. has been with me from the beginning. He and Lynnette gave me my start. Fresh out of community college, armed with an associate's degree in construction management, I was spinning my wheels doing crew work for a home-building outfit out of Bakersfield. That summer I ended up on a job building a new house for O. and Lynnette, who had just tied the knot. She was sweet, funny, true: all the good things. "They say you can't go home again, O., but maybe you can," I said to him when, fresh off his latest divorce, he began mulling the possibility of looking up Lynnette—this was a while back, before he and I hit this rough patch—and he kind of whimpered into the phone like the words had hit some soft spot in him and taken root. So, you know, mission accomplished.

The day I met O. and Lynnette was a scorcher. Middle of the afternoon and I'm shirtless, holding a five-gallon water bucket over my head, my finger on the spout button, alternatively drinking and dousing my face. You know: eyes closed, neck arched, delts and traps taut from supporting the weight of the bucket. A perfect pose even though it wasn't meant to be a pose, which, of course, is what the perfect pose is supposed to look like. I was interested only in wetting my whistle, but in O.'s eyes, I was selling iced tea or lemonade or sports drink. Lynnette told me later that she tingled when she saw me that afternoon, that the sight of wet and shirtless me inspired in her the desire to escort O. back to his Mustang convertible and love him up a little right there on the shoulder of the road. Having that kind of effect on somebody by doing nothing, by just looking like yourself and being thirsty, is hard to beat—it's a quality I try not to take for granted—and because Lynnette and O. are the people who first saw this potential in me, who took the time and made the effort to nurture it and cultivate it, they'll always have me in their corner.

Anyway, no sooner do I put the water bucket down than the two of them are sidling up to me. O.'s slipping his business card in the hip pocket of my Carhartts, asking me have I ever done any modeling, do I have representation, do I belong to a gym, and Lynnette's asking if I'm wearing sufficient sunscreen, how I feel about regularly scheduled haircuts, if I have any hang-ups in regards to full-body waxes. They're both looking at me in the same way, over the tops of their sunglasses, and the two of them seem to be fighting the same grin.

Within a week I have headshots, within a month regular catalogue work. O. and Lynnette put me up in an apartment around the corner from their house, hire me a personal trainer, lease me a car, get me a cell phone, even set me up on a few dates, enough of them for me to realize models shouldn't date models. I eat all my meals with O. and Lynnette. Lynnette's a great cook. The fact that she's beautiful to boot makes me think now that she could've had her own Food Network show. Anyway, we build ourselves into a team, into—I'll say it—a family, and one thing leads to another, which leads to another, which leads to *New Digs for Newlyweds*, and the rest is history.

One of my biggest regrets, O.'s, too, is that Lynnette wasn't there to enjoy the fruits of our labor when *New Digs* came calling. Her and O.'s marriage didn't explode in some melodramatic way; rather, the air just gradually went out of it, like a slow-leaking tire. There were long working hours, long solo trips to visit sick parents, and longstanding fundamental philosophical disagreements about having and not having children. When the two finally split, I worried that I'd be expected to pick a side or be cast as a go-between, but Lynnette drew back from me as she drew back from her marriage. Class all the way. It was a gracious, even chivalrous, gesture. O. got full custody of me.

Now that Lynnette's back in the picture, brightening O.'s future, I wonder if his perspective might change, if he might be reminded that sometimes risks pay off, that sometimes the grass is actually greener, and he might be willing to budge a bit in terms of how he envisions my career unfolding. O. says gravy, but I don't want gravy. Not yet. I don't want *New Digs* to be my last stop. A few film scripts have come my way, and although I thought some of them looked OK, O.'s said he hated them, so as a result I started tinkering around with my own script, but he didn't like even the idea of that. He's used the word "foolish" on a few occasions, which was bad enough, but in one conversation he got loud, talked over me, barked the word "selfish." I'm selfish because I want to explore my potential? Because I'm willing to take an initial pay cut and decrease my visibility in order to try my hand at art? Can sacrifices be selfish?

This was a question I posed to Donna on the night we shared. Yes, this part of our conversation took place in my Motor Coach's steam shower/sauna. You need to see past this detail, though, to get to the essence of what transpired that night: two people in need who were willing to help one another, willing to lend one another their respective ears. Donna was concerned she might've just made one of the biggest mistakes of her life by marrying a makeover project, a closet alcoholic whose love of her, she suspected, was a kind of penance—this is what she told me she was concerned with, and despite all that's come to light, I think I still believe her—and I was wallowing in my identity crisis, worried O. was right, that my acting aspirations were nothing but self-deceiving pipe dreams. Sometimes a steam shower with a stranger is what you need. The shower offers intimacy, the stranger objectivity. I know I felt better afterward. Revived and rejuvenated. By the time we changed back into our clothes, I was telling Donna that her and Larry's love was long-haul love, that he deserved another chance, that she'd invested too much of herself in his betterment to give up so soon, and she was telling me that to give up a dream is akin to dying, that sacrifices can never be selfish no matter how you slice them, and as we went back and forth like this, I began to feel a wave of artistic recommitment and re-inspiration. It's a wave I'm still riding, even as I face the more unpleasant repercussions of the night in question, even as the show and I potentially face accusations of being unsavory, illicit and—this one hurts the most—disingenuous. Even if you don't make your living on reality TV, what's worse than being told you're not real? That you're a phony, a fraud and a sham. That you're imagined. That you're pretend. That you're a liar. Or worse. That you're a lie.

I realize I'm in no position to point fingers, but there have been some recent developments that suggest the *New Digs* research team fell asleep at the switch when they approved Donna and Larry for the show. We're talking major red flags missed. We're talking serious dereliction of duty. Turns out there are holes in Larry and Donna's backstory big enough to drive my Motor Coach through.

For one thing, it now appears that, in order to be together, both Larry and Donna left spouses and children behind. That's a big-time no-no for the show. On top of that, newly discovered evidence points to the fact that Larry and Donna self-nominated, which is a clear breach of the show's rules. We were under the impression that their nominator was Larry's college roommate and best man—the guy wrote a hell of a letter and seemed perfectly credible during the phone interview—but then he didn't show up to the wedding. Larry told our producers that the guy had had a death in his family and had been forced to cancel at the last minute, but now we're thinking that the whole roommate story was probably bogus. No one can find the guy. It's like he never existed.

So things are tough right now for those connected to *New Digs*, from the bigwigs on down. It's hard to know what and whom to believe. If I had the opportunity to deliver a pep talk to everyone, I'd tell them something about how there are no shortcuts to healing, how the process has to start at the beginning, and I'd remind them, first and foremost, of the importance of believing in oneself.

As for me, I can take solace in the fact that my role on *New Digs* is and has always been legit. I pound the nails, saw the boards, sand, spackle and paint right along with the rest of the crew, and when a project's done, the celebratory tears I cry along with the newlyweds when their new house is unveiled are heartfelt and genuine. I even do my own hair because I like how I do it better than how the hair and make-up people do it. The cool way my blond highlights contrast with my brunette soul patch? Totally me. The hair and make-up crew was like, "Please don't," but after I did, they were like, "Actually, not so bad. In fact, very chic," and I was like, "In your face!" but in a positive way.

Probably some people associated with the show, even though I'm friendly with everyone, have taken to thinking that this whole fiasco is my fault. While I can see how they might arrive at this conclusion, I disagree. It's like I told O.: I feel some measure of culpability, but nothing close to full-fledged guilt. He called this semantic bullshit. I called it thoughtful, measured and nuanced. He told me thoughtful, measured and nuanced won't fly with the suits or the lawyers or, heaven forbid, the cops. His advice is deny, deny, deny. As for repercussions and consequences, he told me I should at the very least be prepared to give up the Motor Coach. "Get ready to rack up the frequent flyer miles, Kingsley," he said.

In making this threat, O. was being especially mean-spirited. The reason I have the Motor Coach in the first place—the main reason he was able to get it for me in his negotiations with the network—is because I suffer from aviophobia. I know being scared to fly isn't rational—I know the stats don't bear it out—but the heart fears what it fears. At any rate, while I love O., while I recognize the history we have together, while I understand he and I are much better off together than apart, I'd be lying if I said he hasn't disappointed me with the way he's responded to this crisis. He's said some reckless and cruel things, and while I fully anticipate he'll take them back at some point once this blows over, once we're back at work on next season's slate of episodes, he hasn't taken back anything yet.

Of course, the Larry and Donna episode will never air because of all the deceit and misbehavior. Even before Donna and I hooked up in the Motor Coach, things were heading south. The wedding reception is where things started to get ugly. Too real even for reality TV. We couldn't do our usual sit-down with the couple because Larry was lit, and at the cake cutting, he butterflied the meaty part of his thumb like a thick-cut pork chop. He was lucky the cops were already on the scene because they could rush him to the hospital in their patrol car. They'd been called an hour earlier when, in the parking lot, a couple of Donna's coworkers tangled with a few muckety-mucks from BridgeCo. When one of the officers asked Donna if she wanted to ride along to the emergency room with her husband, she declined. Hard to blame her. With her sloppy drunk groom's thumb-blood splattered over the lace bodice of her gown—I must say that Donna wore the hell out of that dress—she looked like she was in between takes on the set of a slasher movie. Plus, she was embarrassed. Plus, I think she'd already decided that she needed to get away from her new husband for a while to clear her head. Of course, O. and others are of the opinion that this was all part of Larry and Donna's plan. Him getting messy drunk, slicing his thumb, leaving behind his blushing bride in distress. I was their mark, and the two of them were already playing me.

I have a hard time believing this—the paramedic told me the knife hit bone—but O. tells me I'm being naive, especially knowing what we do now about how Larry was on the hook for a couple million in bad real estate deals. Desperate times, desperate measures. Anyway, where we are now is that Larry and Donna are telling O. and the show's producers that unless they get the money they're asking for, they're going to the press to do their damndest to paint whistle-clean, big-hearted, stand-up guy Kingsley Carter as a seducer and spoiler of vulnerable new brides.

Is Donna the first overnight guest I've entertained in the Motor Coach? She is not. Most of the time it's a bridesmaid or a caterer or a bartender or a musician. It's not always women, though. Last season in Lexington, for instance, a bunch of groomsmen and I had a great night sipping bourbon and playing spirited hands of poker. I'm an attentive host. I enjoy company. What you see on TV isn't a put-on. I'm a people person. That being said, I swear it's true that Donna is the first *New Digs* bride I've ever put up for the night.

In the spirit of full disclosure, though, I'd be lying if I said that never before has tension arisen between bride and groom on account of me. Of course, we try not to convey this tension on the show. It's not that kind of show. Besides, the nature of the tension is usually harmless and temporary. Here is a bride flush with emotion; here is a huge, gorgeous house being granted to her, a space for her wifely fantasies to come true; here I am, the emblematic bestower of this new domestic dreamscape. If when she hugs me her arms linger around my broad shoulders a bit too long, if she meets and holds my eyes post-hug a bit too fervently, if her kiss of thanks is closer to my mouth than my cheek, can you blame her? Even if you're the groom, don't you have to cut her a little slack? We're not talking love here. Not the brides on the show, and not the women watching at home who sometimes sneak thoughts of me while making love to their husbands, who buy my how-to books at least in part because of the full-color, step-by-step photographs of me showing them how-to. There are a lot of good-looking men in the world. A lot of beefcake. But how many come with the complementary fantasy of a state-of-the-art backyard patio? A finished basement? Updated light fixtures? Installation of an Empire Tahoe Luxury 36" Heat Circulating Direct Vent Fireplace?

If blame has to be cast, don't blame the bride. Don't blame me, either. Blame Darwin. A fit, handsome man is providing for the woman, and she's responding instinctually. Blame the poor bride's DNA. Blame nature. Blame nurture. Blame her hardwired urge to nest. Blame her biological inclination to be had and to be held.

Environmental champion that she is, Donna didn't approve of the Motor Coach. She called it an oil spill on wheels. The beast has a two-hundred-gallon fuel tank and gets under five miles per on the highway. Inexcusable. I don't approve of those numbers either. What I do approve of, though, and what Donna grew to appreciate in the time we spent together, is the glove leather and rosewood-finished bedroom, the granite-topped kitchenette counters, the surprisingly roomy master bathroom, and the aforementioned two-person steam shower/sauna.

When on a shoot, the show parks me a few miles outside of town, away from the hotels where the rest of the *New Digs* crew stays. For the Battle Creek episode, I was set up at River Oaks County Park, halfway between Battle Creek and Kalamazoo, in a parking lot on the shore of Morrow Lake, which is really a large, dammed up swell of the Kalamazoo River. It's where the oil spill cleanup crews were making their last stand.

When Donna showed up, it was just about sundown. The workers were gone for the day, and other than a security truck that drove by once early on—Donna waved to the guard like she knew him—there was no one else there other than me. The park had been closed to the public since the cleanup efforts had started, but *New Digs* had made arrangements with the powers-that-be to park the Motor Coach there. So Donna knew where to find me. Of course, she did. The only thing I had to promise during my stay was that I wouldn't take any pictures, and I didn't. Besides this rule, the only others I knew of were the common sense ones posted on the sign at the entrance to the park, the ones in existence back when the park was just a park and not an environmental disaster control center. No Hunting. No Fireworks. No Swimming In Undesignated Areas. No Solicitation. No Littering. No Profanity. I swear I broke not a one of these.

When Donna knocked on my door, she invited me out rather than herself in. She told me she didn't want to be alone, but she didn't want to be with anyone she knew either. Then she asked me if I was up for a walk.

As we strolled along the grassy shore of the lake, Donna slipped into tour guide mode. She pointed out and explained to me the functions of the 12,000 feet of containment and absorption boom strewn across the lake, the skimmers anchored here and there along the shore, the fleet of vacuum trucks, the docked air boats, the excavators, and with each piece of cleanup equipment she described to me, her voice grew shakier and quieter. When she stopped talking, I put my arm around her, for comfort, and then we just stood silently on the shore, watching the setting sun glint on top of the oil-sheened water. After a while she put her head on my shoulder, turned her mouth to my ear and told me that the engineers estimated they'd be able to capture ninety percent of the oil at Lake Morrow. "A miracle," she said.

Of course, I then asked her about the rest of the oil, the remaining ten percent, the remaining 100,000 gallons, and Donna broke down. Through tears she told me that when it comes to efforts like this, you do the best you can given the conditions. "You can only do so much," she said. "You can't unspill the oil." I know she was talking literally when she said this, but I also thought then that, in an indirect way, she might've been saying something about her drunk and wounded mess of a new husband.

As she cried on my shoulder, I took the opportunity to share with her my sympathy and empathy for the plight of oil-covered water birds. One thing you can do to reach out to someone who's sad is try to cheer them up, try to get them to leave the sad place they're in, but another thing you can do is go to that sad place with the person. So she knows she's not there alone. I guess this is what I was intending by bringing up the birds, and it seemed to work, seemed to bring Donna around a little. She lifted her head off my shoulder and told me what people don't realize is that, in most cases, it's the petroleum the birds ingest that dooms them. A water bird has to constantly keep its feathers aligned for buoyancy, for insulation. "That's why they're always tending to themselves with their beaks," Donna said. "It's a matter of survival. So oil-covered birds, by instinctively trying to take care of themselves, actually end up poisoning themselves. Death by preening."

If Donna was lying all night, she was good at it. So good at it that I can't help but think maybe she actually convinced herself that the things she was saying and doing were rooted in truth. So in that sense, then, maybe not lying at all. Not only lying.

Of course, it's possible that O. and the others are right. That Donna and Larry were cutthroat deceivers from the word go. That Donna talking with me on the lake shore about the plight of oil-covered birds was part of her and Larry's prepackaged deception. That later, when she entered the steam shower/sauna, she did so with Larry's blessing, even under his instruction.

While I understand this line of thinking, I can't quite accept it. It doesn't quite ring true. When it came time for Donna to leave the Motor

Coach in the morning, she didn't radiate satisfaction or relief. It wasn't mission accomplished. Rather, in her soulful goodbye kiss, I could taste shame and remorse. She wasn't reveling in success. She would've taken the whole night back if she could've. She hadn't been there to do a job.

What I imagine occurred is that Donna spilled her guts to Larry when she got home. I imagine she fessed up and apologized as soon as she walked in the door—I doubt she even tried to think of a good lie to explain her night-long absence—and I imagine that Larry ranted and raved, that they cried together, and that, eventually, out of this shared pain sprung the idea to target me. They needed a villain to rally around, someone to punish instead of each other. We sent them to Costa Rica for their honeymoon, and I imagine them sketching out the big picture of the blackmail plan on the airplane at 40,000 feet—my stomach tightens just thinking about all that empty air below them—and then I can picture them hashing out the details of their scheme while sipping umbrella drinks at the resort's poolside bar.

There's one more reason I don't believe Donna was scamming me—not yet, anyway—that night in the Motor Coach. As things were winding down, right before we went to sleep, I asked her if she might want to read my screenplay. I thought she'd be a perfect reader. As a litigator, enforcement officer and defender of nature, I imagined she knew the world, the real world, in truer and deeper ways than most people, and beyond that, I'd detected over the course of the night her distaste for affectation, fluff and theatrics. She struck me as a straight-shooter, someone who seemed to know quickly and decisively what she liked and didn't like, what was working and what wasn't. I told her all of this and said that if someone like her was interested in what I'd written so far—Act I, thirty pages—I'd feel encouraged and empowered to keep going.

She agreed to read the script, and not only did she read it—with a fierce attentiveness, I might add, breaking only once or twice to look at the ceiling or sip water pensively—but when finished, she offered me spot-on, rigorous, keen-eyed, affirming yet take-no-prisoners feedback. To my mind, you don't make this kind of selfless, honest effort to benefit someone you're swindling. Maybe you read the script, move your eyes over the words, nod and say you like it, but you don't take the time and expend the energy to get into a bona fide back-and-forth script development session. You don't do what Donna did.

Anyway, what matters is, no matter what, I'm coming out of this thing a winner, at least in terms of my art. Donna's critique has served to help me unlock the script's potential. Turns out the key was the female character hanging around the fringes of my plot. The protagonist's love interest. Donna wanted more of her. She said, "OK, I know right now the film's not about the girl. Not just about the girl. And I don't want it to be just about the girl. Can it be a little about the girl, though? A girl like this, it's got to be about her on some level, right? Maybe some pretty major level?" And that's what I needed to hear. Now it's mostly about the girl, and it's good. I might have written myself out of a starring role in the film with the revision I've done, but this could be a blessing in disguise. First I'll walk, then I'll run. I'll cut my teeth on a solid supporting role or two before looking to take on leading man stuff.

As soon as Donna left the Motor Coach, I called O. It was early—between six and six-thirty—but over the course of our years together, until just recently, of course, it's been our habit to touch base every morning.

When Lynnette answered his phone on the first ring, I recognized her voice immediately even though it had been more than ten years. I was, of course, thrilled. Still am. O. was in the shower, so she and I chatted a while. At first she seemed a little shy, a little reserved. I think I woke her up—there were some awkward silences on her end—so I forged ahead and mentioned that I was calling to talk to O. about my screenplay, that I'd been having trouble selling him on the move I wanted to make into film. In response she spoke slowly, seemed to choose her words carefully. She said that sometimes people have to agree to disagree, that whether or not I ended up getting O.'s blessing, I'd still have to do what I had to do. And then Lynnette interrupted herself and out of the blue asked me if I thought she was being stupid for giving things with O. another chance after all these years. She asked me if I thought she was a slow learner.

Her question, how her voice wavered when she asked it, made my heart drop, and I realized that both of us were doing something we shouldn't be doing, putting each other on the spot. We both had things we needed to work out with O., and I didn't want to get to the point where Lynnette and I felt like our respective interests were in competition with each other. Our first conversation in a decade, we shouldn't be making each other feel like monkeys in the middle. With this in mind, I redirected our chat, aimed our words away from the present and future and toward the past, where there was less at stake. In doing this, I had in mind O.'s notion about the difference between weddings and funerals, and it seemed to work.

The mood lightened as we reminisced about when the three of us were young, when everything was new and just beginning. Both of us did the obligatory "If I'd have known then what I know now" thing, but we also re-affirmed for each other how happy those days were. I mentioned to Lynnette the time she and O. took me horseback riding at her parents' ranch outside Tempe, and I reminded her how she'd told me that no man, John Wayne, Michael Landon and Robert Redford included, ever looked better in a saddle, in a cowboy hat, and as I was remembering this, I couldn't help but wonder if trail riding was a tourist option in Costa Rica. Maybe a place where Donna and Larry could ride on the beach, side-by-side through the whistle-clean surf, until they came upon a romantic seaside bistro where they could tether their horses in the shade and unwind with some cold beer and arroz con pollo, and maybe in doing so they could re-find each other. There are worse things that could happen on a honeymoon.

Lynnette responded to my ranch memory by reminding me—she thought she was reminding me—of how she and O. used to tease me about how lucky I was to be good looking because of how horrible the house was that my crew and I had built for them. She called it a money pit and cited the leaky basement, the nightmare plumbing, the shoddy electrical, the cob-job roof. She laughed as she talked, and I did too despite the fact I didn't remember either of them ever mentioning any of this to me, kidding or not. Truth is, to my mind, that house had always been perfect.

BYCATCH

I'm stern-side, leaning over the gunwale, answering nature's call when I see her break the surface. She gets a good five or six feet of air before crashing back into the water. As I tuck myself in and zip up, I'm thinking maybe steelhead, maybe lake trout, maybe sturgeon, but my sunglasses are in the cabin, and the sky's cloudless, and the lake's all shimmers and flashes, a carpet of diamonds, so I can't quite make her out. On her second leap, though, I get a good look and then some. Like how Goliath got a good look at David. Like how Liston got a good look at Clay. Like how in the War of 1812 on this same lake, the Royal Navy got a good look at Admiral Oliver Hazard Perry. By the time I realize she's barreling toward me, all I can do is brace myself and absorb the hit. A cannon ball to the chest.

Next thing I know the fish and I are splayed flat, side-by-side on the deck, the both of us wide-eyed and stunned-still. When the cobwebs clear and my wind returns, I get back on my feet, bend down and wrap my fingers around the fish's thick middle. She gives a half-hearted shiver and flaps her tail once, but her heart's not in it. After her initial protest she just lies there in my hands, slick and heavy like driftwood, her grey, frog-like mouth seemingly the only living part of her. It moves open and closed, open and closed, like she has something she wants to say in her own defense but keeps thinking better of it. Like there's a lie she knows she needs to tell, but she doesn't quite know how to start. There's typically not much to read in a fish's eyes, but there's something in how this one's looking at me that suggests she knows she's not just a fish. As the first Asian carp in Lake Erie, she's a dark harbinger, a tragic omen, a nightmare come alive, a worst fear realized. She's a problem and then some.

When I carry the fish into the cabin, Ian doesn't even look up. He's culling the last of our perch nets—it's the final time he'll do this, although neither he nor I know this yet—and his mind is on finishing up and heading in so he can squeeze in a nap before rehearsal with his band. Pre-dawn, leaving the dock for the day, still picking the remnants of breakfast from his teeth, Ian has his mind on finishing up and heading in so he can squeeze in a nap before rehearsal with his band. On his first day working for me more than twenty years ago—I hired him as a favor to his sister, my then girlfriend, a woman of God—he had his mind on finishing up and heading in so he could squeeze in a nap before rehearsal with his band.

Across the cabin from Ian and the perch, I flip an empty tub right-side-up with my foot and lay the fish in it. The moment she slides from my hands, I get that buzzing sensation up and down my neck and into my shoulder that my doctor tells me is likely nothing serious, but at the same time isn't something I should altogether ignore. He's a man who covers his bases. A quality I appreciate and, up until recently, would've numbered among the positive traits I thought I myself possessed.

In the process of filling the tub with water, I pass Ian six times with a bucket—three round trips from tub to sink—and it's only on the final pass that he notices what I'm up to.

"What do you got?" Ian asks as I pour the last bucketful of water over the fish. He's done picking perch and is slumped on his bench, scratching his belly under his apron. "Salmon?" he says. When the occasional Coho gets hung up in one of our nets, I'll take it home for myself. I used to offer them to Ian before he confessed to me that he doesn't like fish.

When I don't reply right away, Ian takes a second guess. "Catfish?" Then a third. "Bowfin?" I wish catfish. I wish bowfin.

"Asian carp," I say to him. "Asian carp." I say it twice. Enough for two fish.

There's a long quiet moment then. As Ian waits for me to tell him I'm kidding, I retrace in my mind the carp's route. I watch her steer herself from the Mississippi north toward the Illinois River, then the Chicago River, and then Lake Michigan. From there I follow her down the Strait of Mackinac into Lake Huron, and then into the St. Clair River, and then into Lake St. Clair, and then into the Detroit River, and then into Lake Erie. Despite the ecologists' warnings and the engineers' best efforts. Locks and dams be damned.

When I look at Ian, I see that his face is tight and pale, and I wonder briefly if he's going to grab a filet knife and stab the fish dead right then and there, and then I wonder if he moved to do so, if I'd move to stop him.

Ian doesn't kill the fish. Of course, he doesn't. Maybe he should've, though. Or maybe he should've stuck himself. Or maybe he should've stuck me. Maybe, maybe, maybe. I've heard it said that hindsight's 20-20, but experience tells me it's anything but.

As I've just recently resigned myself to being done with fishing, as in retired, the truth of the work that's defined my life seems suddenly less dangerous. It's now over-and-done-with truth rather than current truth. Ian would say I'm in denial making this distinction, but he'd be wrong. I'm not denying anything; rather, I'm finished with everything.

For the last twenty-five years, I've run an illegal gillnetter and trawler out of Conneaut, Ohio, peddling all varieties of fish and fish-like creatures along both the north and south shores of Lake Erie. There's more to the lake than perch, whitefish and walleye, and I've caught and sold it all. Sheepshead, suckers, alewife. Gizzard shad, drum, smelt. My nets yielded no trash, only treasure. The trick is you have to have to know your customers, and I did.

I have a guy in Erie, Pennsylvania, who has for years taken all the burbot I could bring him. He smokes the livers and eats them in hot dog rolls with tartar sauce. By him and others, I will be missed. Another customer of mine in Port Dover, Ontario, has for more than a decade bought all my lampreys. This woman collects and prepares recipes from old 18th and 19th century cook books—to each her own—and one of her favorites is lamprey with blood sauce. She brought the recipe along with her to the dock one afternoon to show me, and I still remember a little of it even though I've tried to forget. "Set a vessel under the lamprey while he roasteth, so to preserve the liquor that droppeth out of him." Since Everett Creech and his buddies at Ohio Wildlife Enforcement told me back in the late '80s that lampreys would soon be "for all intents and purposes" gone from Lake Erie, whenever I pulled one in, I liked to pop its suction cup mouth off its host and break this spooky news directly to its horrendous face. "For all intents and purposes, you're not here right now," I'd say. "For all intents and purposes, you don't exist. Be that as it may, prepare to have the liquor roasted out of you, you fish-sucking sonofabitch." Ian laughed the first couple times I did this, then the next few times he just smirked, then it got to the point where he'd pretend like he didn't hear. I understand jokes get old. That said, when you share a boat with one other human being for six days a week over the course of two decades—nothing else around except sky and water, gulls and fish—I'd suggest you have a certain obligation to respond graciously and appreciatively to your companion's stabs at humor. The least you can do. You do less than the least, I think that says something about your character.

If Ian wants to start accusing people of being in denial about their lives, I'd suggest to him he turn his focus inward. I wonder whose ears he uses when listening to his own band. Ian's spent his entire adult life as a man at war with himself. Avocation versus vocation. Rock-and-roll bar band member versus commercial fisherman. His pastime requires he be late to bed, while his career requires he be early to rise. Ian's war is an absurd one—unjust, even—as he is at best a mediocre fisherman and a bad musician. Bad like sin is bad. Like he and his band should be punished. They have numerous deficiencies, not the least of which is their name, Orange Roughy. Why choose a foreign ocean fish as your moniker when you live on the shores of a Great Lake? Senselessness bordering on insolence. Even more problematic than their name, though, is the group's inexplicable knack for getting worse the longer they play together. Two decades worth of terrible and counting. Now that Ian won't have his day job to hold him back, now that he'll have as much time and energy as he wants for rehearsal, it's both fascinating and sobering to think just how awful he and his bandmates could become.

It's hard to imagine now, but when I first hired Ian all those years ago, it was because I thought there was a good chance he'd eventually end up family. The brother I never had. I thought his sister, Marcia, was my future. She'd just graduated seminary when we met, was working at a small church in Cleveland and set to be ordained as a Lutheran minister. Nowadays, the Lutherans have all sorts of women clergy, but back then it was courageous, even genuinely revolutionary what she was doing, and I admired her for it. I even saw some parallels between what she was doing and what I was doing, starting up my fishing business when the commercial industry as a whole, at least on the American side of the lake, seemed about ready to go belly-up. So it seemed on the surface of things that Marcia and I were a good match, not only in terms of what we did, but also in terms of how we thought. We both liked rooting for the underdogs when watching football together after church—if the Browns were on, this meant most of the time we rooted for them—and after Marcia turned me onto Martin Luther—another underdog, taking on Pope Leo X like he did—we shared an appreciation for him, too. Our favorite quote of his was "Be a sinner, and sin boldly."

Marcia said our admiration of the quote was rooted in its "paradoxical audacity," and this sounded right to me, but eventually I came to understand that the two of us heard Luther's words differently from one another. We saw them zeroing on the respective truths of our individual lives in different ways.

This is how I heard Luther: If grace is going to save you, it's going to save you. In fact, don't look now, but it already has. So it's an act of faith, really, to sin, knowing all the while you've already been forgiven. Given my line of work, this seemed especially poignant. It seemed like a divine green light of sorts, signaling me to keep casting my illegal nets and culling my illegal fish. When I ran this by Marcia, though, she said she thought I was missing something significant about what Luther had in mind, and she said she'd pray for me.

I don't now and didn't then doubt that Marcia was right about me missing the whole truth of Luther's words, but I think she was also missing something in explaining away what he said. She said he was being hyperbolic. Rhetorical. According to her, Luther was saying something outlandish for the sake of getting people's attention, for the sake of planting the seed of a more subtle, nuanced spiritual notion about the infallibility of grace and completeness of God's forgiveness and mercy. "You have to look at his words in context," Marcia said. "After he tells you to sin boldly, he tells you to believe even more boldly." She wanted to put all her eggs in that basket, the basket of belief—she wanted to de-emphasize the part about sin—and I thought her doing so was taking the easy way out.

So Marcia and I agreed to disagree about Luther, and as our relationship went on, we found ourselves doing this more and more. Agreeing to disagree can nip an argument in the bud—it can momentarily keep the peace; it can rescue an evening from unpleasantness—but agreeing to disagree too often can eventually lead to frustration and doubt. That's a truth. Here's another one: When God's the other man in a love triangle, God's not really the other man. When Marcia was assigned a church in Oregon, we were sad to part, but we were maybe a bit relieved, too.

So I kept Ian as a parting gift. His band was just getting together—I think they then called themselves Cataclysm, or maybe it was Calamity; at any rate, just like their music, their names have gotten steadily worse over time—and I never could quite pull the trigger on firing him. I kept telling myself next week, and then next month, and then next season, and then I told myself to wait him out, that he'd quit eventually. I admit now there might've been something else at work. Maybe on some level I liked having him around me everyday because he was a link to Marcia, because I wasn't ready to be completely unlinked from her. At any rate, whatever the reason, it went on like this for more than two decades. No one to blame but myself.

Like most afternoons, there wasn't much conversation between Ian and me as we headed into the dock house with the Asian carp, but we both knew what the other was doing, scanning the water for more of her kind, and we both knew what the other was thinking, that even if we didn't spot any more today, it would be only a matter of time. The way some scientists tell it, the Asian carp will spell the end of the Great Lakes as we know them. The renegade fish will team up with other members of the invasive species army—the zebra mussel, the rusty crayfish, the round goby—to eat and eat and eat everything else into oblivion, leaving nothing but skeleton lakes behind. Two ghost men on a ghost boat full of ghost fish. What it felt like that afternoon.

We'd typically stop to stow our gillnets before docking. About a mile out, just a few compass ticks west of our dock house, I'd anchored a couple crates so they bobbed just beneath the surface of the water, and I hid all my gillnets in them. I needed to play it safe just in case Everett or any of his underlings were waiting for us at the dock. Although still OK for Canadian fishermen, gillnets are illegal in the U.S. The reasons given are that gillnets are indiscriminate in terms of what kinds of fish they entangle—if the fish is the right size to get caught in the mesh, it gets caught, no matter its species—and because of how the fish get snagged in the nets, via their gills, throwing back fish you don't want isn't an option because most of them are already dead or too close to it to make a comeback. Those who defend the law talk about bycatch—they bemoan all the fish the gillnets kill in vain because the commercial fisherman don't want them or use them—but for me there's no such thing as bycatch. I aim to turn everything in my nets into cash, so there's no rational reason for me to abide by this law. To do so, I'd have to abandon all good sense.

Of course, my use of gillnets is only one way in which I'm crooked. Most significantly, I harvest walleye. The legal quota for commercially caught walleye in Ohio is precisely zero. As in none. So on afternoons we're bringing in walleye, in addition to hiding our gillnets, we also have to keep our fish tubs under canvas in the stern of the boat. Any signs of enforcement agents, we have to dump them. Seagull picnic. It's a sad thing to have to do, but circumstances being what they are, I have no choice. While I never a day in my career minded breaking unfair laws—not only didn't I mind breaking these laws, I relished breaking them—I everyday minded the possibility of getting caught.

It all goes back to the '60s and '70s when the sports fishing lobbies and their money convinced politicians that commercial outfits were taking more than their fair share. So we got skunked and screwed. The kicker is that Canadian outfits are still making money hand over fist with gillnets and walleye both. They call walleye "pickerel," but it's the same fish, the same nets, the same lake. A bitter pill I could never see my way clear to swallow.

All this to say that Ian and I didn't even bother stopping to stow our gillnets on the way in that afternoon, and neither of us called ahead to the dock house to ask Tony and Ginger if the coast was clear, and when we finally docked and unloaded our boat—I don't think I've ever been so glad to get off the water—we did so without even a trace of our usual care and vigilance. It's as if we both knew it didn't really matter anymore. Or it mattered less than it ever had before. Or it wouldn't matter for long.

Ian appointed himself to tell Ginger and Tony about the carp—it was on the way out of his mouth as we stepped through the dock house door, before I even had a chance to decide whether I wanted to burden them with the issue or not—so within a couple minutes the four of us were back on the tug, in the cabin, staring at the fish as if waiting for her to tell us how we should proceed.

Ginger and Tony have been with me since the beginning, and there's not a team of quicker, more precise fish cutters out there. The three of us were just out of high school, just beginning to work for Lakeshore Fisheries when the onslaught of regulations put the one-hundred-year-old operation under, and a few years later when I bought my own tug and announced my intention of making a go of it on my own, Ginger and Tony told me they were game. Economic opportunities were scarce in Northeastern Ohio in the '70s, and they were scarce in the '80s, and in the '90s, and they still are today, so the three of us have always considered ourselves fortunate to have each other. I owe Tony and Ginger a lot—the decent run I've had on the lake, I couldn't have done it without them—and it occurs to me that I've lost sight of them and their perspective in all this. My recent actions have had a substantial impact on them, and I haven't to this point thought enough about this aspect of the situation. What's done is done, but that's no excuse. I know this is something I'll need to figure out how to set right. My hope is that the three of us will eventually be able to talk things out and come to some kind of understanding. Even if only to agree to disagree.

Tony and Ginger and I have gotten on well from the get-go, but we've never been what I would call close. They have each other, and that seems enough for them. This is fine, but it's hard sometimes sharing a room with them. Marcia and I went on a double date with them once—this was years ago, of course—but it was really like two separate single dates. With Tony and Ginger, their world sometimes seems to have a capacity of two. I'd walk in the dock house some afternoons—my dock house, mind you—and feel like I was intruding. Like a movie set extra who, in the film's pivotal scene, strays stupidly in front of the camera, ruining what had been shaping up to be a perfect take. Tony and Ginger have this energy that can be fun to be around, but it's not in any way generated for you or by you.

All this said, I admire the two of them. I've never seen them be short with one another, never detected anything between them but tenderness, and while it might sound odd, I think what makes them so good at slicing up fish is their perfect love and camaraderie. They're able to channel it into their work at the filet table. Precision and unity, like those synchronized swimmers at the Olympics. I was present on one occasion when they each nicked themselves at the exact same moment. They dropped their knives in sync, yelped in sync, ran to the sink in sync, and a few minutes later they were back at it, sawing just as quickly and effortlessly as before, except now they sported matching butterfly Band-Aids on their respective left ring fingers. I'll say it. Romantic.

So given the nature of what I knew to be between them, it surprised me when Ginger and Tony disagreed with one another about what should be done with the Asian carp. Tony and I were on the same wavelength, but Ginger sided with Ian, who was of the opinion that we needed to take the fish immediately over to Everett's office at Wildlife Enforcement. He was adamant, and the more he talked, the more Ginger nodded. The two of them acted as if there were no other option. They were flabbergasted when Tony and I balked, telling us that our concerns about Everett using the situation to shut down our operation—a clearly stated goal of Everett's, one which he'd loudly expressed in their presence on more than one occasion—were paranoid.

"This is bigger than you, bigger than Everett," Ian said to me. "Besides, this has nothing to do with his being out to get you. All you have to do here is tell the truth. Tell how the fish literally jumped you. There's no reason to get into what kind of nets we were using. You were taking a whiz." He paused before continuing. "I think you've been lying so long that you're now scared of the truth, even when it's not a threat."

Ginger sensed how this comment hit me, and when she added her voice to Ian's, she did so in a way meant to stifle my building anger. "This whole thing could end up working in our favor," Ginger said. She looked at me intently before continuing, wanting to make sure I was with her. "It'll shift Everett's focus. He'll have a new top priority, Asian carp, so it won't be us in his sights 24–7 anymore. This could prove to be good cover for us for a while. Give us some breathing room."

"Makes sense," Ian said. He was looking only at Tony and Ginger now even though I was the one to whom he was directing his words. "Again, though, the real priority here isn't us. It's the lake. We need to get this fish into the right hands for the sake of the lake. Get her to the people who know what they're doing, whose job it is to deal with her."

To Ginger's point about the carp taking heat off us, Tony and I didn't think for a minute that's how it would work. We knew Everett would find a way to use the situation against us. To Ian's point about getting the fish into the right hands, we weren't even close to being convinced those hands were Everett's. I remembered when I was just getting started, just a kid working for Lakeshore out of Sandusky, I couldn't believe how many of the enforcement officials were unable to identify the species of the fish they were inspecting. And a lot of them weren't only ignorant but also crooked. There was a nonsense regulation about how guys on the boats weren't allowed to take home fish for themselves. It was a wink and smile thing, though. A lot of the guys had families and struggled to make ends meet. They take a few perch home in their lunch pail for a family fish fry that evening, who are they hurting? I remember once Everett got into it with one of the guys, and he ended up making the guy dump his lunch pail. He took the poor chump's perch, and an hour later he was out on the dock eating fried perch sandwiches. Big smile on his face like he'd proved something other than what a horse's ass he was.

Remembering this made me angrier than I'd been all those years ago when it had happened, and although I still had no idea what I was going to do with the carp, I knew what I wasn't going to do.

Before I rushed the fish off the boat, I told Ian, Tony, and Ginger three things. First, they'd earned a week's paid vacation starting tomorrow morning. Second, they'd be fired if they said anything about the fish to anyone before hearing from me. Third, they had my word that I was going to do my best to not make a bad thing worse.

I took the Asian carp home with me that night. I dumped it from the tub headfirst into a pail, added some water, and for the ride home I wedged the pail in between my leg and the center console of my truck. The carp's tail twitched now and then, each time sending some water lapping over the bucket's edge onto my thigh, but it seemed to be an arrangement that the both of us could live with temporarily, and I did my best to take the road slow and steady.

When we got to my house, I carried the carp directly to the bathroom. As the bathtub filled, I sat on the lid of the toilet and held the pail in my lap, and when the tub was two-thirds full, I stood and gently slid the fish in. Stretched out in the clear water, her dark body resting on the sky blue acrylic bottom of the tub, she looked longer and thicker and brighter. I figured maybe thirty inches. Maybe twenty pounds. More of a gunmetal blue than a gray. The thought of a tape measure and scale passed through my mind, but she didn't look up for poking and prodding, and I didn't see the point.

After watching her for a few minutes—I was worried by her stillness for a while, but eventually her fins started waving, and her tail swayed a little—it hit me that I'd given up my shower. I should've sneaked in a quick one before putting her in the tub.

So I grabbed soap and a towel and headed down to the basement to clean up at the utility sink. I then put on clean clothes, grabbed a sandwich and beer from the kitchen along with a half-full bag of corn niblets from the freezer for my guest, and returned to the bathroom to see how she was doing.

The carp's and my story came close to ending at this point because I almost stepped on her. She'd jumped out of the tub and was lying in the doorway, flat on the linoleum like a welcome mat. When I picked her up she fought with more spirit than she'd shown before, and after I wrestled her back into the tub, I drew the shower curtain closed. Knowing the curtain wouldn't do much to hold her after she regained her mojo enough to make another leap—I wondered if her jump had specific purpose, if notions like freedom or suicide were swimming around in her brain—I hustled back down to the basement to see what I could find. I went through the lumber scraps leaning against the wall behind my washer and dryer, thinking I might be able to rig up something with them, but when I spotted my old pup tent rolled up in the corner, I knew I had my answer. I gave the tent a few shakes to rid it of cobwebs and cellar dust, grabbed a couple bungee cords out of the junk drawer in my kitchen and then headed back to the bathroom.

After some wrangling I came up with something akin to a pool cover. At any rate, it seemed to do the job. I left a little opening at the head of the tub through which I sprinkled a few corn nibblets when I was done. I watched the opening for a few minutes to see if she'd go for them, but she didn't seem interested. When I came back twenty minutes later, though—I did some dishes and went outside to towel off my truck seat—the niblets were gone. I went downstairs to get more, and on the way back up I grabbed my radio so I could listen to the Indians game. That's how I spent my evening. The game went eleven innings, and I didn't leave the bathroom until the last pitch was thrown. Longest I've ever sat on a toilet.

It was a little after midnight when the phone woke me. I didn't hear it ring, but I heard the answering machine come on. I just lay there in bed, listening to this voice drone on without being able to make out any words or even figure out who it was talking. I tried to go back to sleep, reminding myself that I had the day off tomorrow, that I could stay in bed as long as I wanted, and warning myself that once I was up, I was up, there'd be no going back—I've always been like this, even as a kid—but my curiosity won out. "No worries," I said to myself as my feet hit the floor. "You can sleep when you're dead."

As I passed the bathroom on the way downstairs to the phone, I thought about checking in on the carp, but I decided to put that off until after I'd had coffee. A part of me feared I'd find her belly-up, and if that turned out to be the case, I'd then be forced to figure out if her demise made my situation harder or easier to deal with, and I thought it reasonable to put off such considerations until I was fully awake. As I thought all this, I found myself tiptoeing down the stairs, taking care to avoid squeaky boards, as if the fish, if still alive, were a sleeping baby. As if I were a burglar.

The answering machine message was from Ian. Of course it was. He said he was sorry to call so late, but this thing was eating him up, and, job or no job, he needed to tell me that he'd decided he was going to Wildlife Enforcement. In fact, he and Everett had an appointment at noon, at which time Ian said he was planning to "come clean." He was calling not only to tell me his plans, but to invite me along. He'd stop by my house at eleven-thirty to pick me up. He said he hoped I'd go with him to "get out in front of everything." He thought it could help me "in the long run."

As I waited for my coffee to drip, I replayed Ian's message four or five times. "Everything." That's what Ian said he was looking to come clean about, to get out in front of. "Everything." That's the word that bothered me most. It sounded like he wasn't talking only about Asian carp. It sounded like he intended his conversation with Everett to be more extensive. My gillnets, my walleye, my out-of-season catches, my second set of books, my Tony and Ginger. At any rate, the fact that I needed to act was becoming obvious, but what to do, how to do it, and who to do it to, these things weren't clear. When was clear, though. Now was when.

When I scooped the carp out of the tub and back into the pail, she didn't fight me, but she seemed none the worse for wear, as if the few hours of rest she'd gotten had steeled her for whatever fate might throw her way. I admired her.

After getting situated in the truck—rather than wedging her against the console again, this time the fish sat with me, on my seat, so I drove kind of side-saddle with one arm draped overtop the pail—we headed to the boat, and once there, after putting the carp in the cabin, I proceeded to the dock house to collect what I needed.

I started big, wrestling my filing cabinets onto the boat, and worked my way down from there. Boots, bibs, smocks and aprons. Tubs and weights, scales and nets. At one point I paused to transfer the carp from the pail to the one of the tubs, let her stretch out a little, and during this breather

I thought about grabbing Tony and Ginger's knives. I'd bought them after all. I finally decided, though, that they didn't belong to me anymore. Of course, they didn't. Tony and Ginger had earned them and then some. I was about to leave the two of them in a tough spot, and it made no sense to leave them in a tougher spot. Knifeless. The two of them might want to try to go cut for somebody else. There were no fishermen left, but maybe they could get on behind the counter at one of the local grocery stores.

I'd leave nothing for Ian, though. There was a radio in the dock house that he sometimes fiddled with. Tony and Ginger liked the AM oldies station, but Ian would always change it to the FM album rock station. He'd ask if it were OK, but he'd ask as he was already in the process of doing it. So I grabbed that radio—it was the last thing I grabbed—and once we got out into the lake, it was the first thing I pitched overboard.

On the way out to the dumping spot, I'd stopped to gather my net crates, and they went over after the radio. I weighed them down so they'd sink. They were followed by everything else. Took me a while. I had to stop and rest more times than I care to admit. I'd spent more than two decades hauling fish out of the lake and thought that was tough work, and it is, but after spending just under an hour doing the opposite, throwing things in, I wondered if I'd ever labored so hard.

Everything not bolted down went in. Everything but the carp. I wasn't yet sure what I was going to do with her, but my conviction was that dumping her back in the lake was the coward's way out, the fool's way out. I wouldn't be solving a problem, I'd simply be washing my hands of one. Passing the buck. Besides, the fish was starting to grow on me. I was beginning to see that the two of us had some things in common, and I was newly reminded of something I'd known for a long time, that survival of the fittest was a rigged and unwinnable game no matter how good a cheater you were. Everett and a lot of other people, maybe even a lot of good people, wanted the same fate for me as they did for the carp. For better or worse, the fish and I shared enemies. This was a hard fact to ignore, so I decided not to ignore it. Partnerships have been based on less.

After my work was done and I had us headed back in, I could already tell I'd be sore the next day. The filing cabinet drawers had been heavy, and the net crates had been heavy, and I was getting that buzzing up and down my neck and shoulder again. Maybe just an almost old man's aches and pains that would lessen with a few days' rest. Maybe a pinched nerve that would only get worse over time. Maybe I was sneaking up on a stroke. At any rate, I wasn't feeling my best. Truth be told, though, I couldn't remember the last time I had. Fishing's a hard line of work, and getting busted up is part of the deal. After a decade or so, you realize keeping track of exactly what hurts and when it started hurting doesn't make sense. Same thing with the boats. Early on, when my tug was new to me, I knew the story behind every ding and scrape, but after a while, I stopped keeping score.

Thinking along these lines put a lump in my throat. As I steered my boat through the dark water, I knew my time behind her wheel was coming to an end, and I felt a wave of regret over never having given her a name. In those first couple years, Tony, Ginger and I had volleyed a few ideas back and forth, but we'd never decided on anything except that we didn't want to keep the name the former owner had given her— *The Bottom Feeder*—so on the licensing and registration paperwork, I'd just written "fishing tug," and then enough time passed so that giving the boat a proper name would've felt odd. Like I'd be forcing something that didn't need forcing. At any rate, my sudden sentimentality aside, it was probably good in the end—we were getting there, I realized—that she turned out to be just an unnamed boat. I didn't know where or with whom she'd end up next. Maybe I'd donate her to a museum—she was a relic for sure, one of the last American commercial fishing boats on Lake Erie—or maybe I'd sell her to some guy with significant disposable income, some accountant or supervisor of accountants, who would take his friends out for beery Saturday afternoons on his real live old-time fishing tug, and off her deck they'd catch walleye—get them while they last—which they'd have mounted on plaques to hang in their studies over their display cases full of golf scramble participation trophies. Or maybe she'd end up as scrap metal. Or maybe I'd take her out one night soon—not tonight, though—and sink her.

I thought through these scenarios for a while before realizing I wasn't just thinking them through, I was talking them out. Since no one was around, I concluded I must be talking to the boat herself. Or maybe it was the carp I was addressing, and the boat was eavesdropping. This kind of nonsense in my head, you'd think I would've known enough to clam up, but I didn't. I kept at it. Sorting out pros and cons. Distinguishing greater evils and lesser evils. Weighing causes and consequences. I blathered on and on. Neither boat nor carp could've gotten a word in edgewise even if they'd wanted to.

Still a couple hours shy of dawn, the carp and I found ourselves back in the truck, heading south. I kept her in the larger tub for this last leg of her journey—in my fervor, I must've thrown her pail overboard—so she was riding shotgun in the passenger seat, and between the seatbelt and my sore right arm, I was doing my best to keep her from having too rough a ride. We stopped at a 24-hour Gas 'N Go on Route 7, where I filled up my tank and bought one of those breakfast sandwiches you heat up in the microwave. It wasn't that bad. I ate as I drove, occasionally half on purpose, half by accident dropping biscuit crumbs into the tub, which the carp seemed to appreciate.

When we got to Andover, we headed to the Pymatuning Reservoir. I steered us through the parking lot down onto the grass, as close to the water as I could get. In trying to hoist the carp and tub out of the truck, my shoulder went wet noodle on me, and I spilled the fish on the ground. She had a fit in the grass—it was still dark, so I heard and felt her flipping more than saw it—and I eventually had to hold her in place with my knee on her tail so I could grab her under the gills. In the process she bit me pretty good. Even now, looking closely at my wrist, I can see the bracelet of teeth marks. Carp typically have soft mouths and blunt teeth, so I can't help but be impressed, and I can't blame her for lashing out. I'd put her through a lot—not only her, but every fish I'd ever come in contact with, and I had at least one more fish after her whose day I aimed to ruin—but I'd like to think that, in hindsight, maybe a part of her regretted getting rough with me. Once she realized what my intentions were, after I'd waded into the reservoir up to my knees and laid her gently in the cool water, gradually loosening my grip on her and then, finally, giving her a little nudge away from shore, I'd like to think she wished she could've had that moment back when she sunk her teeth into my skin. I'd like to think this. I'd like to think a lot of things.

Over the Pennsylvania border, at the Linesville spillway, people gather along the edge of the reservoir to throw bread at carp. These carp aren't of the Asian variety, of course—they're just your run of the mill trash fish—and the way they huddle en masse on top of each other by the spillway delights people for whatever reason. The blanket of them is thick enough that ducks get in on the act by running across the backs of the fish in pursuit of the bread. The park service encourages the spectacle, even going as far as to sell stale loaves at a concession stand right on the water. I don't get the attraction, but I suppose it's harmless enough. At any rate, as I stretched out on top of a nearby picnic table for a breather, I hoped my carp would steer clear of the spillway. I hoped she'd stay in Ohio, find a nice mud-hole, and live out her years in peace. I knew she wouldn't be a real threat to anything there in the reservoir—she couldn't go anywhere, and one Asian carp wasn't going to put a dent in the fish population of such a heavily-stocked body of water—and I didn't think anyone or anything would be a threat to her either. If she ended up on the wrong end of a boy scout's line, he'd probably get his picture taken and then throw her back. Or maybe he wouldn't throw her back. Maybe she'd swallow the hook and despite the boy scout's best efforts she wouldn't make it. Or maybe the little sonofabitch would clean her and eat her. Earn his Asian-carp-on-a-stick-over-an-open-fire merit badge. At any rate, her fate was her own now, apart from mine, and this was a relief, although not as much of a relief as I thought it might be.

I lay still on top of the picnic table, not asleep, but not quite awake, until the sun showed up. As the sky brightened and I could see the water from where I lay, I sat up and looked and listened for jumping fish, but I didn't see or hear anything except frogs and birds and the growling of my own stomach. That first biscuit sandwich had gone down easy. What I should've done was buy two.

So that's the next thing I did. I returned to the Gas 'N Go—it was a different cashier now, so I didn't have to feel sheepish—and I bought two more biscuit sandwiches. When I finished the first, though, I knew I sure didn't need the second. Evidently, given the sleep-deprived, churned-up state I was in, the number of biscuit sandwiches needed to satisfy my hunger was a hard thing to get right. I'd taken a couple cracks at it and was 0 for 2. At any rate, besides the biscuit sandwiches, I also bought a hot dog, one of those shiny, wrinkled numbers from the rollers over the heat lamp, but the dog wasn't for me.

My next stop was Wal-Mart. I headed to sporting goods, told the kid behind the counter that I needed a rod and reel, that I'd trust him to do my shopping for me, and that I'd be waiting for him at the register. When he started asking me about open-faced vs. close-faced reels and medium action vs. fast action rods, I held up my finger and told him I didn't care. When he asked if I'd be in need of a license—he said he could set me up right then and there—I pretended not to hear him, and he didn't ask again.

The last time I'd been fishing with a rod and reel was with Marcia. Our first date. I asked her to go on a picnic with me, and she said she would under two conditions. First, she was going to make all the food. Second, I was going to have to work for my supper. I agreed, having no idea what was on her mind.

When I showed up at her house that Saturday afternoon, things quickly became clear. Along with a jug of iced tea and a basket of egg salad sandwiches and chocolate chip cookies, she brought along with her an old fly rod—she called it a pole—and a milk carton full of night crawlers. She said she'd heard through the grapevine that I was a fisherman, and she wanted me to take her out and show her the basics because she'd always thought it sounded like fun. I laughed at first because I thought she was kidding, pretending to not understand what kind of fisherman I was, but I eventually realized she meant what she said.

We cast around for about an hour in an old farm pond she directed me to before I finally got up the nerve to tell her how much I hated it. To spend the work week pulling in fish by the net load and then to spend a rare day off catching them one at a time didn't make much sense to me, especially when I'd rather be eating egg salad sandwiches and drinking iced tea. She got mad like I thought she might, but not for the reason I expected. She told me she felt stupid and wanted to know if that was what I intended, not speaking up and telling her the truth until half the afternoon was gone. I'll never forget what she did then. She raised the fly rod over her head with both hands, parallel to the ground like it was a barbell, and threw it as far as she could into the pond. Neither of us said anything for a few seconds. We just stood on the bank watching the rod float on the surface. I took a step toward the water thinking that the chivalrous thing to do would be to swim out to retrieve it, but she grabbed my arm and asked me politely to please not make her feel even more foolish than she already did. She laughed then, which was a great relief to me, and I laughed, too, and she loosened her grip on my arm, but she didn't let go.

From that point on, if there were ever a lull in conversation, or if one of us sensed that the other was cranky or melancholy or too much in his or her own head, we'd say, "You want to go fishing?" It was one of my favorite things that we said to each other because we'd turned a memory of misunderstanding into something funny, and I thought at the time that if the two of us could do that, we could maybe do anything.

Back at the reservoir, I baited my hook with a chunk of hot dog and, with my spent right arm hanging uselessly at my side, cast wrong-handed over and over again into a shady pool between a submerged log and a patch of lily pads about thirty feet offshore, where I imagined a heavy, hungry catfish or sturgeon or, who knows, maybe even a carp, lay waiting for breakfast. Almost an hour of this. Nothing. So I put a fresh hot dog chunk on the hook, forsook the shady hole, and cast as far as I could into the open, sun-kissed water, like some idiot who didn't know anything about how fish thought and lived, and wouldn't you know it, ten minutes later I was landing a catfish. Not a record-setter by any means, but a good five or six-pounder. I threw him in the back of the truck, and after another twenty minutes I had a second smaller one to join him, and then I was done. I hoisted the rod over my head with both hands, parallel to the ground like a barbell—my right shoulder burned like it had a bullet in it—and flung the rod as far as I could into the water.

Ian arrived at my place a few minutes earlier than he said he would, but I was ready for him. I'd already fired up and cleaned the grill when I heard the doorbell ring. I shouted to him to come around to the backyard, and by the time he was on the scene, the catfish steaks were already lined up and sizzling.

There were no words at first. Ian just kept looking at the steaks on the grill, and then at me, and then at the steaks on the grill, and then at me. "What are you doing?" Ian said finally. "What have you done?"

"Lunch," I said. "My retirement lunch. For I'm a jolly good fellow. Bon appetit. By the way, you're fired."

Ian surprised me with what he did next. Like he was channeling somebody else. Bad and bold. If he were ever able to summon up this kind of chutzpah on stage, maybe he and his band could get themselves moving in the right direction.

Ian rushed me, wrenched the spatula out of my hand—had he known how sore my shoulder was, I wonder if he would've been gentler or rougher—and flung it into the yard. He poked his finger in my chest, smack-dab on the spot where the carp had landed the afternoon before. "You've made a huge mistake," he said.

"Plenty of them," I said.

He said, "You'll regret it."

"Undoubtedly," I said.

Then it was over. Ian disappeared around the corner of the house, and I heard his car door slam, and I heard him hit the road. His tires squealed, like he was making a getaway.

I turned my attention back to the fish, which was coming along nicely. I squeezed on some lemon, sprinkled on some salt and pepper, and then wandered into the yard to fetch my spatula. It wouldn't be long at all before the steaks needed flipping.

CURB APPEAL

After the second house of the morning—a three-story colonial with six bedrooms, two fireplaces and a Jacuzzi tub on the back deck—Clay's inclined to set Klecko straight, re-establish parameters and price range. He tells this to Michelle on the front lawn where they wait for Klecko, who's stayed behind in the house to use one of the three bathrooms. Three-and-a-half counting the commode in the finished basement. Take your pick.

"Please relax," Michelle says to Clay. "Please be patient. We're just getting started. We'll get to the shacks and shanties eventually. In the meantime, let's just go along with it. It's fun. I think it's fun."

"Some fun," Clay says. "Maybe you should sit with me on the way to the next place. I need help getting in the spirit."

"Poor guy. You lonely back there?" Michelle smiles through a fake pout and takes Clay's hand. "Seriously, though, wouldn't that be weird? Kind of rude? Gerry alone up front chauffeuring us around? We could switch, though. You want to switch? You want shotgun?"

"Forget it," Clay says. "I'm good."

"Ready, kids?" Klecko says from the front porch. When Clay and Michelle turn, he smiles and claps his hands three times in front of his face. Like he's killing bugs or trying to wake himself up. Like a short burst of applause is in order. Like he's anticipating something great. Like something great has already happened.

Alone in the back of Klecko's Suburban, Clay's out of the loop. Up front, Michelle and Klecko chat about home warranties and buyers' assistance programs, casement windows and pocket doors, high-efficiency furnaces and updated wiring, stand-alone garages and in-ground pools. These are the kinds of things Clay imagines they're discussing. Problem is, between the noise of Niagara Falls Boulevard's stop and start traffic roaring through the truck's open windows—Klecko's air conditioning is reportedly on the fritz—and the staticky, booming voices coming out of the rear stereo speakers, Clay can't hear Michelle and Klecko. Instead, it's *The Spike and Abe Show* on AM 660, The Voice of Western New York Sports, a program which consists of the two hosts talking over each other and yelling at their call-in listeners, and even though it's late July, the main conversation topics are football and hockey. The Bills and Sabres. The shtick is supposed to be that Spike and Abe are an odd couple. Spike plays the excitable ex-jock who's all heart, no head, and Abe plays the sarcastic, cerebral stats nut. They zing each other accordingly. Clay thinks the callers are the most interesting part of the show—Phil in Lackawanna, who wonders what the Sabres can do to amp up their power play, or J.J. in Amherst, who thinks the Bills should trade up and draft a quarterback—but Spike and Abe never let the callers talk for long. They have their provocative riffs and passionate tangents to get to. They have their hasty generalizations and snap judgments to pronounce. Clay finds himself anticipating the respite offered by the not nearly frequent enough commercial breaks.

Clay could be assertive. He could take matters into his own hands, request the windows be closed and the radio turned off, but he doesn't. Partly out of pride—he shouldn't have to ask—but partly out of wariness, too. Clay knows himself. If he were included in the loop, it wouldn't be long before he'd be looking for a way out.

Michelle knows Clay, too, and Clay knows Michelle knows. She's not maliciously ignoring him; rather, she's giving him a pass, letting him off the hook. She understands house hunting isn't his thing, and she can tell he has misgivings about Klecko. The man sports a handlebar moustache and juggles two cell phones. He wears a leather newsboy hat, fingerless driving gloves and a white-gold man bracelet. Call Clay shallow, call him unhip, but he'd feel more comfortable if Klecko looked more like a real estate agent and less like a bookie, or an undercover narcotics cop, or mob muscle.

Earlier this morning, in the parking lot of the Red Roof Inn where Clay and Michelle are staying, Klecko said, "Don't call me Klecko, call me Gerry, short for Gerald, Gerald with a 'G'," and he suggested that the three of them all ride together in his truck. Michelle accepted before Clay could answer. If Clay were out to find fault, he could blame Michelle for jumping the gun, or he could blame himself for being slow on the draw. Either way, what was sacrificed was the privacy necessary to speak frankly, to pow-wow, to compare notes and strategize between houses. Of course, Clay understands, in theory, that everyone here is on the same team. Klecko is Clay and Michelle's agent, their advocate, not their enemy. You don't for-mulate strategies to deal with your advocates. Still. It seems Klecko might have a strategy. Clay wonders if splitting up husband and wife between front seat and back seat is a commonly employed technique. A trade secret. A tactic. Like what cops do with perps. Clay's seen the shows. Two suspects, two interrogation rooms. You play the scumbags off each other until one cracks.

After spending the rest of the morning tromping through a series of sub-urban McMansions in Sanborn and Wheatfield and North Tonawanda, Clay gathers from the snippets he overhears—no one says anything to him directly—that the plan for the afternoon is to get lunch and then hit Black Creek Village. There's a house for sale there that looks great on paper, and, what's more, it's within shouting distance of Clay and Michelle's price range, so Clay feels like things are looking up. Like Klecko and Michelle are finally ready to get real.

Clay's been ready, has lived through more than his fair share of real-ity in the last few months. He and Michelle are moving to Niagara Falls from Harrisburg because of Michelle's new job, and Clay's been nothing but supportive from the get go. Michelle's told Clay how much she appreci-ates the way he's responded to all the upheaval. The school district's budget cuts and his resulting pink slip on the one hand, and on the other hand, Michelle's burgeoning career, her great new opportunity. She waxes as Clay wanes. A lesser man, well, who knows? A lesser man might allow jealousy to worm its way into his heart. A lesser man might allow himself to feel like a lesser man. Clay has this lesser man in him—who doesn't?—but so far he's managed to beat the lesser man down. Clay's tough-minded. Clay's for-ward-looking. He knows he and Michelle are fortunate her new job came along when it did. Her head registrar's salary at the community college in Niagara Falls will be thirty percent higher than what she earned as an assistant registrar in Pennsylvania. Not that their budget won't be tight—it will be until Clay finds work—but he'll land something soon. Clay's not the kind of guy who won't land something soon. Things could be worse. These days, things are a lot worse for a lot of people. The reason Clay and Michelle can even think about buying a house is because prices and mortgage rates have dropped so low, and prices and mortgage rates have dropped so low because of underwater loans and foreclosures. One person's burst bubble is someone else's golden egg. When Clay reminds himself of this, of other people's hardships, of those who have it tougher than he does, it makes him feel better, but not in an altogether good way. Fact is, feeling better like this often makes him feel worse.

The restaurant Klecko pulls into has two signs in opposite corners of its parking lot. One says "Whirlpool Diner," and the other says "Breakfast–Lunch–Dinner 24/7." The buildings surrounding the restaurant look like they've been long abandoned, including, across the street, a weather-beaten Niagara Falls Tourist Information station. The small booth is hugged tightly by weedy vines and covered with incoherent graffiti, and a half-dozen seagulls take turns hopping on and off its sagging roof.

There are empty spaces everywhere in the sizeable parking lot, but Klecko's got his eye on one in the row closest to the door, between two other big trucks, and he's hell-bent on backing his Suburban into the space. As Clay waits for things to play out—when Klecko finally hits pay dirt on his fourth attempt, Michelle gives a little cheer—he realizes he was never asked what he'd like to eat. Clay will usually eat just about anything—Michelle probably conveyed this fact to Klecko—but, still, some direct consideration would've been nice. The gesture would've been appreciated. On the short walk from the truck to the restaurant—Clay follows a few steps behind Klecko and Michelle—he wonders if he'll be allowed to order for himself. He wonders if he'll have permission to get something off the adult menu.

As it turns out, instead of menus, the restaurant's fare is scrawled in chalk behind the cash register. The chalkboard is huge. Nearly wall-to-wall, nearly floor-to-ceiling. Pizza, subs, soups, pasta, broasted chicken, pancakes, omelets, milkshakes, burgers, hot dogs, fish fries, curry bowls, Buffalo wings, chili, burritos, lo mein, egg rolls, open-faced turkey and meatloaf sandwiches, beef-on-weck, ribs and an all-you-can-eat salad bar. Clay's impressed.

"Lunch is on me," Klecko says. He places one hand on Clay's back and the other on Michelle's. "You kids save your money. I hear you're in the market for a house."

"You don't have to do that," Clay says.

"It's not about have to," Klecko says. "It's about want to. The Whirlpool is my favorite place to take clients. Can't go wrong here. The only thing they don't have is sushi. You want sushi, you're out of luck. You want sushi, I brought you to the wrong place, and I apologize."

"I do love sushi," Clay says.

Klecko's smile fades but then reappears, even bigger than before, when Michelle reaches around him to slap Clay's arm. "Behave," she says.

"Just kidding," Clay says. "Not about loving sushi. I do. But this looks great."

"They have calamari," Klecko says, pointing at the chalkboard. "They have crab cakes."

After placing their orders at the counter, Klecko, Michelle and Clay claim a booth at the rear of the dining room. There are plenty of open seats—Clay wonders where the lunch rush is, wonders what the lack of lunch rush might say about the place—but by the time they have their food in front of them, the dining area has filled considerably, and they all agree how lucky they are to have missed the log jam currently forming at the counter.

"Perfect timing if I do say so myself," Klecko says. He then bows his face to the table and closes his eyes. Clay thinks the man's going to say grace. "I love food," Klecko says before inhaling deeply. "I love eating."

"Amen," Clay says.

"What do you have there?" Michelle says to Klecko. She's already taken a bite of her BLT and has leaned over Clay's plate to admire his shrimp fried rice. "Looks to me like a UFO," she says. "Unidentified food object."

"Ha! That's good," Klecko says. "'Round these parts, this is what's called a garbage plate. A Western New York specialty. Especially Rochester, but you can get a good one here, too. You have your macaroni salad, tater tots, beef patty, red hot, white hot, and fried egg covered in chili sauce, cheddar cheese and diced onions. This piece of white bread on the side is your flavor sponge. You use it to mop up the juice."

"I don't use it to mop up anything," Michelle says. "No offense, but your lunch alarms me."

"Actually, ma'am, I am offended," Klecko says as he sticks two consecutive forkfuls of food in his mouth. Clay and Michelle watch him chew and swallow. "You're being close-minded about the local culture, and I'm a native. You're casting aspersions at something near and dear to my heart." Klecko points the business end of his fork at Michelle and winks. "Believe me, it's good stuff."

"Looks like you're really enjoying it," Clay says.

"So no kids yet for you two, huh, Clay?" Klecko says. "What are you waiting for, an invitation? I'm kidding. Maybe in the not too distant future, though, right? Michelle tells me you're looking for a house you can grow into."

"Right," Clay says. He looks at Michelle, who grins sheepishly at her plate. "Having a family's in our plans."

"That's fabulous," Klecko says.

"It's exciting to think about," Michelle says, rubbing Clay's arm. "We just want the time to be right."

"Sure," Klecko says. "You want to have your ducks in a row. Clay, your bride also tells me you'll be looking for work when you guys land here. For what it's worth, I've been wracking my brain trying to come up with some leads for you."

"Oh," Clay says. "Well, I appreciate that."

"Not so fast," Klecko says. "I'm afraid I haven't been able to come up with much. If this were a few decades ago, I could set you up. Right along the lake in Buffalo there used to be a lot of good jobs. A couple of my brothers worked down there at the Buffalo Color plant. At one time they were the largest supplier of indigo dye in the world. You wearing blue jeans? Chances are the blue came from Buffalo. Or used to. The jeans you would've been wearing thirty years ago. Anyway, my brothers are retired, and I don't know how active the plant is anymore. A few guys I went to school with worked right next door at Airco. Industrial gases. They sucked air out of the atmosphere—with big hoses, I guess?—separated it into oxygen, nitrogen and whatever else—I want to say argon?—and then they sold the gases. Genius, right? Making money off air. Pulling money out of the air. Literally, right? Anyway, again, my buddies are all retired, so I'm not sure about what's what over there now. Seems lately everything's going the wrong way, right? Layoffs. Downsizing. I suppose the Chinese have us beat on air, too. Air and its components."

"It's tough out there," Clay says, "but I'm sure I'll find something."

"Even right here in the Falls there used to be Nabisco," Klecko says. "Hooker Chemical, too. One stretch along the Robert Moses Parkway used to be called Chemical Row because of all the plants over there. Jobs, jobs, jobs. Anyway. Now they're gone, gone, gone."

"Actually," Clay says. "I'm a teacher. So I'll probably just apply to local school districts. See how that goes."

Michelle drops her hand onto Clay's knee. "Clay's a great teacher," she says. "His students loved him."

"Sure," Klecko says. He unwraps and slides a straw into his tumbler of Mountain Dew even though there's one in there already. "Gym teacher, right?"

"Phys. ed. Right," Clay says.

"So how's it work when teachers get laid off?" Klecko says. "What are the logistics? They go by seniority? Subject? If you don't mind me asking."

"Right," Clay says. "Seniority and discipline. In my school they cut back the librarians and art and music teachers to part-time, and they laid off a reading specialist and two phys. ed. teachers. Those were the logistics."

"We'll be a nation of obese, uncultured illiterates," Klecko says.

"God bless America," Michelle says.

"I used to love gym as a kid," Klecko says. "Used to look forward to it. Climbing the rope? I used to love that. Kids need gym, right? That break from learning. All work and no play doesn't work."

"I wouldn't say students take a break from learning in phys. ed.," Clay says.

"It's a different kind of learning," Michelle says.

"Sure," Klecko says. "Aerobic, anaerobic, isometric, isotonic. I don't know if you can tell or not, but I work out. I have to, right?" he says, and he points both forefingers at his plate. "Look how I eat."

"I'd rather not," Michelle says, and she laughs. "That sounded mean, didn't it?"

"Hey now," Klecko says, "remember I'm the one paying here."

Clay figures there must be more than two thousand calories sitting on Klecko's plate. A whole twenty-four hours' worth of food. Eat that stuff every day, you'd have to run a few half marathons a week to break even. Klecko doesn't look too bad for his age—he's got good arms and shoulders, a good chest—but Clay would advise him to spend less time on the bench and more time on the treadmill. He could stand to mix in a salad once in a while, too. Maybe skip dessert here and there, switch to diet soft drinks now and then. And he should drink more water. Everyone should drink more water. That's something that kids in Clay's phys. ed. classes heard from him all the time. Sure they had fun, but along the way they learned a little nutrition. Body wellness. A little anatomy, a little biology. Not a break from learning by any stretch.

"All right," Klecko says. "Getting down to business here. The house in Black Creek Village we're going to see this afternoon." He looks at Michelle and smiles. "First things first. Just to get this out of the way. After all the testing they've done, nothing. Absolutely nothing conclusive. No issues whatsoever as far as that goes. Second, most importantly, the price is right on this house. I mean, it's a steal as listed, and I know for a fact we have a motivated seller, so I bet we could even inch them a little lower."

"Testing?" Clay says.

"All clear," Klecko says. "And, again, on top of that, a motivated seller."

"Testing for what?" Michelle says. "All clear of what?"

"Hey," Klecko says, leaning across the booth, wagging a finger at Clay. "Didn't you do your homework? You were a teacher. You should know better."

"I didn't know there was an assignment," Clay says.

"Ha!" Klecko says. "Seriously, though. No worries. This is ancient history. We're talking '70s, early '80s. There was an industrial waste issue in the southeastern corner of the city. A lot of hullabaloo. Really bad for this area, all the negative attention. Anyway, long story short, the EPA and President Carter stepped in and got it taken care of. You two probably don't even remember Carter, do you? He was between Ford and Reagan."

"Is this related to Love Canal?" Michelle says. She looks at Clay. "That's over and done with, right?"

"Exactly," Klecko says. He rips a corner off his slice of bread and smashes it between his thumb and forefinger before putting it in his mouth. "Here's the scoop. More than a hundred years ago, this guy Love started digging a canal from the Niagara River—he had big ideas about hydroelectric power—but he didn't get very far. Only about two miles inland before he ran out of money. So humans did what humans do. Made the best of it. For the next half-century or so, the trench served as a dump. A necessary evil. Industry and the military used it for a while, and, of course, some of the stuff they dumped wasn't great stuff. Surprise, surprise, right? The city got a lot of flack. Hooker Chemical, too. They're Occidental now. They either changed their name or were bought. I'm fuzzy on the details. The blame game, though. I don't play it. People back then didn't know what we know

now, right? Anyway, what got dumped got dumped, and people did what people do. They lived their lives. They built houses and schools, raised their children and fought wars. In the '70s, after a snowy winter and wet spring, some of the stuff in the dump started resurfacing. No one's fault. Blame the weather. Blame the passing of time. Things happen. Not everything buried stays buried, you know? Anyway, people saw this suspicious stuff in their backyards, in their basements, and they panicked. Can't blame them, right? The key is, though, that it was taken care of. Those who wanted to move got to move on the government's dime, and the chemicals were cleaned up. That would've been it except that the media turned it into a whole thing, you know? It portrayed the people in the neighborhood as victims, as symbols. A person's not a symbol, right? One expert even suggested that what was really making people sick wasn't the chemicals, but the stress caused by all the rigmarole. The protesters, the TV cameras, the doomsday headlines. Anyway. Here we are in the 21st century, right? Lucky us. Lord knows we have plenty of our own problems to deal with. Last thing we need to do is look backwards, dredge up old ones. That's my take on things." Klecko picked up his Mountain Dew, nudged the two straws out of the way with his nose, and drained it.

"But what does this have to do with the house we're going to see in Black Creek Village?" Michelle says. "Black Creek Village isn't Love Canal, is it?"

"You hear anything I just said?" Klecko drops his fork and reaches across the booth to cover Michelle's hand with his. There's a smile on his face. "I could've sworn you were sitting right there when I said Love Canal is gone. Over and done with. The houses were razed, and the disposal site was recapped and fenced off."

"If I'm understanding correctly, though, you're telling us that Black Creek Village is in the vicinity of where the dump was," Clay says.

"Lookit," Klecko says. "It's perfectly understandable for you to have questions. If you didn't have questions, there'd be something wrong with you. I guess I'm just a little surprised you didn't look up this info on your own before today."

"You gave us a list of houses," Clay says. "We didn't think about cross-referencing their addresses with chemical dumpsite locations."

"Let's take a step back," Klecko says. "Let's take a breather. I sense you're getting spooked about something you shouldn't get spooked about. Maybe that's my fault. You know what? Rather than me running my big mouth anymore, I think the best thing I can do for you is get you over to the house. A picture's worth a thousand words, right?"

"I guess we can't really know what's what until we see it," Michelle says.

"Exactly," Klecko says. "And what's nice about the location is you're like three, maybe four blocks from the river. There's a boat launch right there at Griffin Park. You guys have a boat? You want a boat? The price you'll be getting on this house, you'll be able to afford one. You a fisherman, Clay? You could catch your own sushi."

"I am not a fisherman," Clay says.

"I'm with you," Klecko says. "Boring as hell, right?"

When they get up to leave the restaurant, Klecko has a plan. He and Michelle will go to the cash register first, and then after a few minutes, Clay will go up to pay for his lunch separately. "I have two coupons, see," Klecko says as he hands Clay one of them along with some cash, "but there's a one coupon per table limit."

"So I pretend like I wasn't sitting with you?" Clay says. "I pretend like you and my wife had lunch together, and I was sitting by myself?"

"They don't know who's married to who," Klecko says. "We'll meet you out in the parking lot."

"To whom," Michelle says. "Who's married to whom." She looks at Clay and shrugs. "Want me to stay with you? You and I can go up together."

"Sure," Klecko says. "Either way."

"Forget it," Clay says. "I have to hit the restroom anyway."

"OK, good," Klecko says. "That'll be good. That'll work."

In the men's room, Clay pitches the coupon in the garbage. Later, though, outside in the parking lot, he tells a different story. "The cashier wouldn't let me use the coupon because she saw me sitting with you," Clay says. "She crumpled it right in my face."

"Wow," Klecko says. "That's petty, right? I mean, that's ridiculous."

"She was none too happy," Clay says. "She told me I should be ashamed."

"Rules are rules are rules are rules," Michelle says.

On the drive to Black Creek Village, Klecko leaves the radio off, the windows up. Clay holds his hand up to the vent above his head. Air conditioning's working like a dream.

Klecko's playing tour guide. He points out the Summit Place Mall, where there's a Save-A-Lot. "This might be the closest grocery store to you guys," Klecko says. "And Sears and Bon Ton are still in the mall. Everyone else left, but there's a rumor that a group from Toronto might move in and try to do something."

Klecko pulls into the parking lot and takes a whirl around the circumference of the mall. As if Clay and Michelle were in the market for retail space. Even if they were, Clay would pass. The parking lot's in bad shape—one big pothole—and Clay's put in mind of a ghost town. Things are too quiet. Seagulls outnumber cars, especially behind the grocery store where they take turns dive-bombing the overflowing Dumpster. Nearby, a stock boy in a red apron sits on the loading dock and tosses a chunk of his lunch to a fat straggler, who catches it in mid-air like a good pet.

When they pass a parked security vehicle, Klecko waves, but the guard doesn't wave back. "That hombre doesn't look too happy, but security guard wouldn't be a bad job, right, Clay?" Klecko says. "If the teaching thing doesn't work out right away, I mean. You'd have to be viligant, though. You're the eyes and ears."

"Vigilant," Michelle says. "Not viligant."

"What's viligant?" Klecko says.

"Viligant's what you said," Michelle says. "It's nothing."

"If you say so, Daniel Webster," Klecko says.

"I'm the word police," Michelle says. She turns around and smiles at Clay. "Right, honey? Grammar, too. I'll get you for can and may. I'll get you for I and me."

Klecko looks in the rearview at Clay. "You're a lucky man," he says.

"How are we doing?" Clay says. "We getting close?"

"Yep," Klecko says. "We just turned onto River Road. The Niagara River's over there on your left, and this is Griffin Park. I told you about the boat launch." Klecko pulls into the driveway of the park and does a slow loop around the parking area. "There are a few walking trails here," Klecko says, "and some picnic tables. People come to exercise their dogs or to get some peace and quiet on their lunch hours."

"What's over there?" Clay says. At the edge of the park stands a high barbed wire fence. It runs from the road all the way to the water.

"Reclamation area," Klecko says.

"Part of Love Canal?" Clay says.

"Short answer, yes," Klecko says. "This is what I meant, though, about a picture being worth a thousand words. I mean, look at this park. Great, right? A lot of neighborhoods would love to have a park like this."

"But what it's next to," Michelle says.

"Lookit," Klecko says, pulling the Suburban back onto the road. "You kids are going to do what you kids are going to do. I understand that. But think about this. You're worried about next to. This is the 21st century. Where can you live where you're not next to something? Good people live next to bad people. Good neighborhoods are next to bad neighborhoods. Good countries are next to bad countries. You can drive yourself crazy worrying about next to."

Michelle doesn't turn her head to look at Clay—Klecko's talking, so this would be rude—but she does reach her hand back toward her husband, and she leaves it there in mid-air until he meets it with his hand, and then she squeezes. Clay doesn't know if she's doing this for his sake or for her own. The squeeze could be Michelle trying to reassure Clay, or it could mean Michelle's looking for reassurance. About how things will be OK if they love the house in Black Creek Village and end up buying it. About how things will be OK if they pass on the house. About how something better will be sure to come along.

"What's great about this house you're about to see are the windows," Klecko says. "They're all dual-functioning. Very convenient."

"Dual-functioning?" Clay says.

"Sure," Klecko says. "You can see in them, and you can see out of them."

"Groan," Michelle says. "Real estate humor."

"Dual-functioning doors, too," Klecko says. "You can go in and out. And all the stairways. Up and down."

Stuck in the lawn next to the For Sale sign is an Open House sign. Surprising for an afternoon in the middle of the week. "Indication of an owner who's getting itchy," Klecko says. "This baby's ripe."

Michelle stands on the sidewalk next to Clay. She cranes her neck back and uses one hand to shield her eyes from the sun. "Is that a metal roof?" she asks. "They last forever, right? Forever's a plus."

Clay likes the roof, too. He wouldn't have had the guts to choose the color—it's a bright green—but it really pops. The surrounding houses have traditional black and brown shingle roofs, and Clay likes how the metal roof stands out. He also likes the idea of living in a brick house. If Klecko mentioned the house was brick, Clay doesn't remember. At any rate, the place definitely has curb appeal.

There's one other couple touring the house, and they're just finishing when Klecko, Clay and Michelle come in through the living room. The couple has twin babies in tow. The father hauls one in a carrier strapped to his back, and the mother has the other in a sling over her shoulder. The open house host, a woman who looks to be in her '50s, can't take her eyes off the babies, can't stop smiling at them, not even as Klecko introduces her to Clay and Michelle.

When the other couple leaves, Klecko tries to make small talk with Eva, the open house host—Clay sees from the nameplate Eva wears that she and Klecko work for the same realtor—but Eva seems reluctant. She smiles politely as Klecko talks—he tells her they're fresh from the Whirlpool where he introduced Clay and Michelle to the garbage plate—but she makes a point of strolling away from him to the opposite side of the room, where a coffee table is set up with a platter of cookies and a punch bowl.

"Tell you what," Eva says when Klecko stops talking. "Why don't I take Michelle and Clay through the house? Gerry, you can take a break. Just hang out down here and greet visitors. Feel free to help yourself to the refreshments."

"Sure, OK," Klecko says. "These two are probably sick of my yammering anyway." He makes his way over to the table and plucks a cookie. "Ginger snaps," he says. He picks up a cup of punch, dunks the cookie and then pops it in his mouth. "I'll hold down the fort," he says.

The house is nice. It's not perfect—the kitchen's on the small side, and Michelle's not crazy about the layout—but there's a newish furnace in the basement, a lot of storage space in the well-insulated attic, and on the second floor, Clay likes the size of the bedrooms, and Michelle likes the newly remodeled master bath. There's some strange wallpaper here and there, and one of the bedrooms has only one electrical outlet, but these are the kinds of things you can address after moving in.

"I don't know if Gerry told you how good the asking price is," Eva says as she shows Clay and Michelle the linen closets in the upstairs hallway, "but it's pretty amazing. With the money you're saving, you could update the electric and get started on some of the cosmetic improvements you might have in mind. Anyway, a house like this, it's a real opportunity," she says. "That's how I look at it."

"It has a lot going for it," Michelle says. "I like the roof. And that corner bedroom would make a great nursery."

"There's a little one on the way! That's wonderful," Eva says. "Congratulations."

"No, no," Michelle says, and she smiles. "Not yet. But it's in our plans." She looks at Clay. "It's a factor in our thinking."

"You're concerned about the history with Love Canal, I'm sure," Eva says. "That's understandable, of course. Frankly, that's why the price is what it is. Location, location, location. Were this house, say, ten or twenty blocks north, the price would be considerably different."

"That's a point," Clay says.

"I think about it like this," Eva says. "What I said before about the house being an opportunity? Part of what I mean is that whenever a house sells in this neighborhood, it helps the people who live around here move on from what was. A new generation, you know? Maybe that's sappy. But just by living here, just by getting up in the morning, going to work and coming home at night, you'd be participating in the ongoing healing process."

"Interesting," Michelle says. "Food for thought."

"Anyway," Eva says, "my two cents."

When Michelle decides she wants to take one more pass through the bedrooms, Clay dismisses himself to look at the backyard. He sneaks out the side door so as to avoid Klecko, who's still hovering over the cookie platter, laughing into one of his cell phones and dialing on the other.

A few toys line the fenced perimeter of the yard. A Nerf football. A plastic dump truck and bulldozer. A one-armed robot. Clay turns around, heads through the sideyard to the front of the house. When he hits the sidewalk, he hangs a right.

While upstairs in the attic, Clay had seen through one of the dual-functioning windows another stretch of barbed wire fence. This reclamation area is only a half-block away from the house. When Clay gets close enough to read the sign behind the fence, "Glen Springs Holdings Company," he inhales deeply, but he doesn't smell anything other than cut grass and the faint smell of cigarette smoke. A hundred feet from where he's standing, there's a guard house at the closed main gate, where two men in hard hats lean on a pickup truck. Smoke break. When they notice Clay, they stub out their cigarettes and get in the truck. Their slamming doors startle a nearby rabbit, send it scurrying under the fence toward Clay, but when it gets to the sidewalk, it freezes, turns tail, and ducks back under the fence again. It finally stops to hide behind what looks like a short, mushroom-shaped chimney sticking a couple feet above the ground. A vent of some kind, Clay figures. They're scattered here and there over the freshly mown lawn. Whatever's buried here needs to breathe.

The truck takes off slowly, following the tire tracks along the perimeter of the fence. Maybe Clay should think about a new line of work after all. How hard could it be? Guarding someplace no one wants to get into anyway? He has both eyes and ears. He can be vigilant. Viligant, too, if need be. What's more, he could walk to work.

Back at the house, Klecko's standing on the front porch, holding the Nerf football from the backyard. Clay gets the sense Klecko's been waiting for him. When he gets close, Klecko tosses the ball at him, but the throw's short. The ball bounces off the top of Clay's shoe.

When Clay's retrieving the ball, Michelle comes out the front door. "Hey," she says to Klecko, "Eva's looking for you. She wants to know what you did with all her cookies."

Klecko snickers and claps his hands in front of his face. "I'll touch base with Eva later. You kids are probably just about ready to get back to the motel, right? They have a pool there? You could have a swim. Then maybe a nap. You guys have some thinking to do, right?"

After they're all in the truck, though, Klecko announces he'd like to make one more quick stop. He drives only a couple blocks before pulling into another park, this one made up of five or six ball fields. The placard on the backstop of the first field reads "Welcome to Cayuga Little League." Klecko drives to the end of the lot, to the last field, where there's a practice going on. A gaggle of boys in sweatpants and crooked caps fielding grounders and pop-ups. In the stands sits a spread-out group of parents, some watching the boys, others busying themselves with their cell phones.

Klecko gets out of the truck, and Clay and Michelle follow him to the fence. Klecko bends over to pinch a long blade of grass and sticks it in the side of his mouth. "I thought it would be good for you to see this place. Someday maybe, right? Little Clay Jr. They have softball, too. Little Michelle

Jr. They could walk to practice. We were talking about next to before. I just wanted to show you something else you'd be next to."

"Shortstop's got an arm," Clay says.

"Coach probably has him pitch, too," Klecko says. "He's twice the size of the other kids. The intimidation factor."

Beyond the field, at the end of the parking lot, there's a short pedestrian bridge spanning a small creek. Klecko strolls to the bridge, and Clay and Michelle follow. "This is 93rd Street, and over there is Cayuga Boulevard," Klecko says. He spits the blade of grass over the bridge's rail into the creek and then takes a ginger snap out of his pocket and pops it into his mouth. "Got a few more cookies stowed away if either of you are feeling peckish."

"I'm good," Michelle says.

When Klecko looks at Clay, Clay raises his hands. He means, "No thanks," but Klecko thinks he means, "Yes, please," and he flings a cookie. Clay ducks, and the cookie soars into the creek.

"You sure you're a gym teacher?" Klecko says.

"You surprised him," Michelle says. "He wasn't ready. No fair."

"I didn't want it," Clay says. "I'm still full from lunch."

"Plus the sun was in your eyes, right?" As Klecko laughs, one of his phones rings, and when he sees who's calling, he rolls his eyes at Clay and Michelle before answering. "Eva!" he exclaims into the phone. "Been too long. What can I do you for?"

Michelle takes Clay's hand and leads him a few steps further onto the bridge. "Well?" she says quietly. "What are we thinking?"

"I don't know," Clay says. "We could always rent for a year. Get the lay of the land before we put down roots."

"Sure," Michelle says. "We could do that." She drops Clay's hand and pinches the bridge of her nose. "We'd probably have to put some of our stuff in storage."

"Or we could pull the trigger on this one," Clay says. "The price is right."

"There's what we can afford to do, there's what we can't afford to do, and there's what we can't afford not to do," Michelle says.

"OK, great! I'll be sure to pass along that message!" Klecko says into the phone as he turns back toward Clay and Michelle, and he shakes his head and smiles after hanging up. "Sorry for that interruption, kids," he says, "but Eva wanted to make sure I mentioned to you two that if you have questions about property taxes or schools, she has that info handy. Guess who else has that info handy, though? I do. It's in the truck, safe and sound in the glove compartment, and when I drop you guys off at the motel, you'll have it in your hands. That was my plan all along. I am your agent after all. Eva has her clients, and I have mine."

"That info will be helpful," Michelle says. "Thanks."

"You have to factor in everything, right?" Klecko says. "That said, you have any idea which way you're leaning?"

"We need to talk it out," Michelle says. "Make sure we're on the same page."

"Listen. I hate to be nosy, but I had one ear on you guys when Eva was talking at me, and I thought I heard the word 'rent.' Is that what I heard?" Klecko says. "You're not sure you want to be homeowners?"

Michelle looks at Clay, bites her top lip. "We have a lot to discuss," she says.

"Well," Klecko says, "that's a bit of a kick in the pants." He turns to face the creek for a moment before spinning back around. "If Eva told you guys that you could work with her, that she could get you some kind of special deal apart from me, well, just to let you know, that's dirty pool. One agent moving in on another's clients. She shouldn't have done that. It's unethical."

"She absolutely did not do that," Michelle says.

"She has a bit of a reputation for being forgetful," Klecko says. "For forgetting things like who brought who to the dance."

"Who brought whom," Michelle says. "But no. Eva didn't say anything about us working with her. She didn't even give me her card."

"Well, OK," Klecko says. "All right then. That's good to hear. Sorry about talking out of school, but with Eva…. Well, there are just some people, you know?"

"So back to the motel now, right?" Michelle says. "I'm whipped."

"Sure," Klecko says. "I'll get you that tax and school info, and then you kids can confer. Maybe sleep on it. I have to say, though. Please hear me on this. Renting? Not a good move. Might as well light your money on fire. Might as well flush it. Might as well stuff it into a barrel and send it over the Falls."

"We shouldn't think of our mortgage as debt, right?" Clay says. "We should think of it as an investment."

"You said it, not me," Klecko says, and he nods as he passes another ginger snap between his lips.

"Also, don't look now, but here comes your future," Clay says. "You should say that to us."

"I know what's holding you back," Klecko says. One of his phone rings, but he ignores it. "You're hung up on the past. You're still on Love Canal. But every place has a past. Focus on the present. Black Creek Village. Focus on the future. What I was trying to convey by showing you those kids up there playing ball. Your line of work, I thought you'd get it."

"I do get it," Clay says.

"Lookit. It would be a mistake for you kids to think of your first house as just a house. It's more than that, right? Isn't it more than that?"

"It's a sanctuary," Clay says. "You should tell us to think of it as a sanctuary."

"Or a haven," Michelle says. "I like 'haven.'"

"Not bad," Klecko says. He flicks a ginger snap high into the air with his thumb, cranes his neck back and catches it in his mouth. "You guys should get your real estate licenses," he says as he chews. "It can be rewarding work. Not that different from teaching, Clay. In the sense that you help people. And you two as a tag-team? You'd clean up."

"Or a refuge," Michelle says as she takes Clay's hand in hers and squeezes it again, this time tightly enough to make him wince. "You should tell us to think of our home as a refuge."

DEVIL'S NIGHT

It's Halloween Eve, so the ballet students at En Pointe Dance Academy of Marietta are allowed to wear trick-or-treat costumes in lieu of their usual leotards and tights. For Joseph's daughter Chloe, who'd earlier that afternoon had a party at school, this means two costumes in one day.

A few weeks ago, Chloe's teacher sent home a note explaining that each fourth grade student would be assigned a costume based on a local environmental theme. On party day, in addition to dressing up, students would be expected to report to the rest of the class on their costumes. One kid went as a pawpaw, another as hemp, and there were more than a few extirpated or endangered species, including an Allegheny woodrat, a timber rattlesnake, and a fawnsfoot mollusk. According to Chloe, all the costumes were lame, but they were all better than hers. She went as fly ash, a toxic carcinogen, a byproduct of coal-fired power plants. Chloe had tried to get her assignment changed, but the teacher had stuck to her guns. All that Joseph and Chloe's mother, Nan, could come up with in the way of a costume was to streak her face with grease paint, powder her hair and dress her in dirty clothes.

So for her ballet class costume party, the aim is to go with something more fun. Nan went the store-bought route, left work early to hit Party City. So Chloe is now some sort of spotted jungle cat. A cheetah or leopard or ocelot. The package isn't species specific. At any rate, although not exactly what Chloe had in mind—she'd been thinking ladybug or Lady Gaga—it beats fly ash, so she seems content enough with the getup. What's more, she's come up with a new persona—if not altogether cute, then acute—to complement her new look. Chloe's not just a jungle cat; she's a snobby jungle cat with a not half bad British accent. Joseph's unsure of the connection between costume and character, and when he inquires, Chloe raises her chin and answers, "It's hardly your place to question." When Nan laughs, Chloe senses carte blanche. Asked what she wants to eat before class, she orders biscuits and jam with a spot of tea and announces she'll take her meal in front of the telly.

Joseph drives Chloe to ballet on Thursday evenings because it's only fair. On Mondays Nan carts Chloe to Brownies and often stays for the entire two-hour meeting to lend a hand, so Joseph knows he's getting off easy. And he likes the time he and Chloe spend together in the car. On the road, she's apt to slip into singing mode—melody and lyrics improvised on the spot—and when she's stuck on a verse, Joseph is called upon as a resource for rhyming words.

On this evening's drive to dance class, though, there's no singing. More than an hour after donning her costume, Chloe's still copping continental attitude. The game is that Joseph is her chauffeur, and they're en route to a high society costume ball. When Chloe asks Joseph about road conditions, he reports it's getting slippery. Not quite November, but already the first snow of the season is falling—looks like there's a little ice mixed in, too—and now, at dusk, it's beginning to stick to the roads. Last year, Joseph remembers, it rained all fall. Southeastern Ohio didn't get even a whiff of snow until Christmas week.

"No more accidents, Jeeves," Chloe says. "I won't abide any more accidents."

In response, Joseph looks in the rearview mirror, raises his eyebrows and sticks out his tongue.

"Eyes on the road, Jeeves," Chloe says. "You can be replaced, you know." Then she breaks character and cracks up, pleased with herself.

The dance school lobby is crammed as usual: dancers accompanied by their mothers, older sisters, grandmothers, babysitters. Joseph has on occasion seen other men at the dance school, but they're few and far between. Even the owner and director's toy dachshund—perpetually rolling onto its back, shamelessly inviting belly scratches from the crowd—is female. The air in the dance school lobby is, even in late fall, warm and humid, dense with the odors of female feet, perspiration tinged with baby powder, and floral air freshener fanned in from the constantly opening and closing door of the single closet-sized restroom. The sign on the door reads "Femmes." The toilet seat never gets raised, and there's always a line. To keep the line moving, the girls are instructed, counterintuitively, not to wash their hands at the sink. Instead, when they re-emerge into the lobby, antibacterial sanitizing gel is squeezed into their palms, and they're asked by the gel-squeezers, "Why didn't you go at home like I told you?" and the girls answer, "I didn't have to go then"—logic that's hard to argue with—and then they rub their moist hands together in front of their noses, trying to decide whether or not they like the smell.

In the ten minutes he spends in the dance school lobby just prior to and after Chloe's classes, Joseph, despite his average size, can't help but feel oafish, can't help but sense that the presiding opinion in the room is he's taking up more than his fair share of space. He pins himself to the wall by the door, leans his head and shoulders back, and works to keep his movements to a minimum, his gut sucked. He tries to look only at Chloe, although sometimes he can't help but sneak a glance at the dog. He tells himself not to, but this is equivalent to telling oneself not to think of a pink elephant, of a rage-driven pink elephant with dangerous intentions. The dog hates Joseph, and if its eyes meet Joseph's, it's reminded of this hatred. The dog charges Joseph, skids to a stop at his feet, barks and snaps at his crotch. The dog doesn't bully anyone else at the dance school, only Joseph. If Joseph reaches out a hand to the dog, palm down and slowly like you're supposed to, it gets even louder, and if Joseph tries to sweet talk the dog, it interrupts its own barking and snapping with a series of wheezy, wet growls. As far as Joseph can tell, everyone in the dance school lobby understands he's done nothing to deserve the dog's wrath, but they kind of blame him, albeit silently, anyway. The opposite of grace.

Each time the dog's turned on Joseph, Chloe has come to her father's rescue. She gets between the dog and her father and squeezes one of the dog's squeaky toys, or tosses the toy in the air and catches it, or holds the toy in front of the dog's snarling face and then hides it behind her back and asks the dog where it went. When the dog finally succumbs to Chloe's charms, when it shuts up, forgets Joseph, and allows itself to be led by Chloe to the other side of the lobby, all the women in the room look meaningfully at each other. Joseph can't discern the precise meaning of the meaningful looks, and he can't tell if Chloe's embarrassed or pleased by the situation. She's always wanted a dog, has always been made to understand she's not getting one.

This evening, just prior to Chloe's class's scheduled start, another girl, a fairy of some sort with glitter on her face and tinfoil ribbons in her hair, says something to Chloe that inspires a full-throated roar and raised claws. The fairy drops her wand and runs away squealing with Chloe in pursuit. This turns out to be a game that all the girls in the lobby want in on. The dog, too. Chloe's on her third manic lap around the room when Joseph steps in, intercepts her with a forearm around the waist, tells her to cool her jets. He has to raise his voice a little, not out of anger—what's there to be angry about?—but to be heard over the giggling, shrieking and barking. He'd detected some disapproving looks from the other adults in the room when the chasing was at its peak, but now that he's put a stop to it, there are other disapproving looks, maybe even more pronounced ones. Like now he's a bully whereas moments before he was merely irresponsible and inattentive.

There are worse fathers. If Joseph's not just being paranoid, if these women in the dance school lobby really are passing judgment on him, he'd like to tell them to consider the big picture for hell's sake. He could offer examples. At the third grade spelling bee last spring, Joseph sat next to a guy cheering on his son with whiskey breath. Ten o'clock in the morning. And there's the father who lives three doors down from Joseph, Nan and Chloe. Seems nice enough, but he's clueless. He cruises the neighborhood on his ten-speed with his eighteen-month-old daughter in his lap. This is the same guy who can't get garbage day right. Pickup is Wednesday. He'll put his cans out Thursday, and they'll sit on the curb for a whole week. The one day he got it right this past summer was July 4th, but because of the holiday, the pickup schedule had been pushed back twenty-four hours, so even when he was right he was wrong. Plenty more where these characters came from. If going back a few years is allowed, if personal history is fair game, Joseph could tell some stories on his own dad. What kind of father, grumpy about the price of glasses, accuses his kid of faking poor eyesight? Taxes his kid's allowance? Fills his sick son's Christmas stocking with aspirin and menthol cough drops? Kids don't get irony. Sardonic, edgy humor doesn't work with children. Looks and feels the same as meanness to them. You have to know your audience.

When Chloe's class is finally called into the studio and begins to clear out of the lobby, just before Joseph makes his exit, as he holds the door open for a just-in-time arriving Little Red Riding Hood and her mother, the dog shoots the gap between mom and daughter, disappears through the door into the dark. Little Red Riding Hood's mother spins frantically and runs a few steps after the dog, calling its name, Clementine—whenever Joseph hears the dog's name, he realizes he's forgotten it—then she whirls back around, grabs her daughter's hand, and rushes past Joseph into the studio. "Miss Linda! He let Clementine out!" she exclaims, and when she returns to the lobby, she has Miss Linda in tow, and the two are rushing over to where Joseph still holds the open door.

"What happened?" Miss Linda asks. She's wearing her usual teaching outfit, but a black plastic mask covers the top half of her face. A leotarded Lone Ranger with shapely calves and perfect posture.

"He's not allowed out?" Joseph asks. "He won't come right back?"

"She. No, she won't come right back, which is why I ask everyone to please take special care when entering and exiting the building." Miss Linda says this like it's something she always says, is sick of saying. Like it's something she can't believe Joseph doesn't know. A maxim. A capital 'T' truth. But all this is new to Joseph—he had no idea the dog was a flight risk—and he's not sure whether to feel indignant or stupid.

"I'll track him down," Joseph says. "Go ahead with class. I'll get him."

"Her," Miss Linda tells Joseph. When she pulls off her mask, the elastic band breaks. "Perfect," she says. She gestures as if to toss the mask aside, but then at the last second doesn't let it go. A woman's prerogative.

"Clementine probably won't want to go to him," Little Red Riding Hood's mother says to Miss Linda, and then she turns to Joseph. "What with how he antagonizes her."

"I don't antagonize her," Joseph says.

"Right." Little Red Riding Hood's mother flings her hands over her shoulders and rolls her eyes back. "It's the dog's fault. It's Clementine's fault she's disappeared."

Joseph feels his face warm, his stomach fall. He lets the door swing closed and raises his hands to chest-level, pats the air in front of him. "No one's fault. This was an accident."

"Accidents seem to follow you around," Little Red Riding Hood's mother says.

"I'll be right back," Joseph says calmly. He looks at Miss Linda whose eyes are shut, whose hands are folded tightly under her chin. "I'll be right back with Clementine."

For parents who wish to observe their daughters' classes at En Pointe Dance Academy, the best place to be is on the outside looking in. There's a large picture window at the front of the building. When the weather's warm, observers cluster on the sidewalk—some even set up lawn chairs—but once heavy jacket weather rolls around, they take turns pulling their vehicles into the row of parking spaces closest to the window, and they splinter off into groups of four and five to keep warm. Some drivers run their vehicles for the duration of practice, a full ninety minutes of idling. "Zero miles per gallon," Joseph once overheard the driver of a Chevy Tahoe say. "If my husband knew, he'd kill me."

Joseph is kicking the bushes alongside the dance studio in hopes of flushing out the dog when a woman cracks open the window of her idling Escalade to tell him she saw Clementine cross the road and head into the field. "Poor baby almost got hit," the woman says. "How'd she get out?"

The driver's window is on its way to closing before Joseph can even begin to respond. Rhetorical question.

The small cornfield across the road from the dance school is mostly mud, spotted here and there with the wreckage of bent, brown stalks and picked-clean cobs. You raise corn; you rear children. Joseph hears the voice of Miss Abernathy, his third grade teacher. Sees her oily face and hair, her smudged glasses. She was the first teacher he didn't like, maybe the first person he'd consciously decided that about. You rear children. He remembers thinking how stupid the right way sounded, how he'd rather say it wrong.

From where Joseph stands on the edge of the field, squinting into the dark, there's no sign of Clementine. He imagines there's now enough snow on the ground that, if the moon were out, he'd be able to track paw prints, but things as they are, he's left to guess. Pressing forward into the field, his route is determined by his attempts to keep his shoes as clean as possible. Every dozen steps or so he stops to listen, whistle, scan the dark field.

Just as he reaches the tree line at the end of the cornrows, Joseph hears barking. Ahead of him and to the left. To the east? At any rate, the woods. He hears human voices out there, too. He can't make out specific words, but the voices are high and chirpy. The tone and cadence people use with children and animals.

To transition from field to woods, Joseph has to step over a thigh-high barbed wire fence he doesn't notice until running into it. Nailed to a tree on the other side of the fence, there's a sign that Joseph can't read until he's right on top of it. Walking over to check it out, his guess is "No Trespassing," but he's wrong. "No Hunting." Trespass all you want.

Joseph walks the dense tree line for a few minutes, doubling back here and there before choosing a point of entry. There's no trail as far as he can tell, so he gingerly picks his way from tree to tree, blindly negotiating roots and rocks. Just as he thinks he hasn't heard any barking or voices in a while, he hears both, and then a whiny engine. Not enough snow on the ground yet for a snowmobile. Maybe a dirt bike.

Joseph continues trudging toward the noise until he sees a single headlight bouncing his way. A few moments later the light's shining directly in his face, and he holds up both arms, crossing and re-crossing them over his head. Like a referee or traffic cop. Like an island castaway signaling a plane.

When the vehicle sidles up a few trees away, Joseph sees it's one of those fat-tired, three-wheeled all-terrain cycles. There are two helmeted people onboard, but Joseph doesn't see a dog. The two helmets seem to be talking to each other as the ATC idles. The driver's neck is craned around, and the passenger is hunched forward. It's difficult to tell who's doing the speaking, who's doing the listening.

When the driver cuts the engine, he and his passenger dismount and approach Joseph side-by-side. Both walk stiffly, a bit bowlegged, as if they've been riding the range for a spell.

"Hey there," the driver says, removing his helmet.

When the passenger's helmet comes off, a ponytail pops out, like a magic rabbit. "Hunting pooch?" the woman asks Joseph.

"Right," Joseph says. "You seen him?"

"We tried to get her to come to us, but no cigar," the driver says. "Did you say 'he'? My wife was calling her 'she.' Anyway. You raised him well. Doesn't trust strangers."

"Isn't it your kid you don't want trusting strangers?" Joseph says. "Don't you want your dog to be OK with strangers?"

"Depends, I guess," the driver says. He switches his helmet from his right underarm to his left underarm. "We don't do kids or dogs. We do cats."

"You don't raise cats so much as wait on them," the woman says.

"I've heard that," Joseph says. "So did you happen to see which way she was heading?"

"So I was right, she is a she," the woman says, and she punches the driver in the shoulder. "Thought so. But yeah, she was on the dirt road heading toward the river, toward the cemetery. She looked like she knew where she was going, so we figured she was on her way home."

"I'll catch up to her," Joseph says. "Thanks. Big help."

"I hope it's OK us tooling around here," the driver says. "We just got the trike today and were anxious to take a spin. Usually we'll be out at my brother's place with it—he has some property over near Zanesville—but, you know, I didn't see any posted signs back here, and it's still early, so I didn't think the noise would bother anyone."

"If you're trespassing, I am, too," Joseph says. "Only sign I saw said 'No Hunting.'"

"So then you're the one outside the law," the woman says. "Hunting pooch. I could make a citizen's arrest here and now."

"Letter of the law, I guess that's true," Joseph says. "Please don't, though."

"Geesh, Kay," the driver says. He swings his helmet back onto his head mid-chuckle. "You ready?"

"Just yanking your chain," the woman says to Joseph through clamped teeth. She holds her hair band in her mouth as she gathers her hair into a fresh ponytail. "So what's her name?"

"The dog?" Joseph says. "What's the dog's name?" And then it comes to him. "Clementine," he says. "Those little tangerines."

"Thou art lost and gone forever. Dreadful sorry, Clementine." The woman doesn't sing the song; she says it, and then she groans. "Shoot. Dropped my hair band."

"Come on, Kay," the driver says, taking a few steps back toward the ATC. "You have two or three hundred extra hair bands at home." There's still friendliness in his voice, but there's now a hint of impatience, too. Joseph gets the impression that the driver has some experience waiting on this woman.

"I'm coming," the woman says, crouching to feel around in the snow and mud. "Don't get your panties in a bunch."

"You know what?" Joseph says, reaching into his hip pocket. "I happen to have a scrunchie on me." He holds it out to her. "My daughter's. She has approximately two or three hundred extras, so you're welcome to it."

"Wow," the woman says. "Abra cadabra." She stands, takes the scrunchie, and brings it to within a few inches of her eyes. "Fancy," she says. "I traded up."

"Look at that," the driver says, and he raises his arms like someone's scored a touchdown. "Happy ending. Let's make tracks."

The woman winds the scrunchie into her hair and puts her helmet back on. Joseph watches the couple walk back to the trike and waits for them to take off, but they don't. Instead, the woman climbs off the ATC again, digs through a saddlebag on the rear of the vehicle, and then strolls back toward Joseph. When she gets within arm's reach, she hands him a flashlight. "We thought you could use this," she says.

"Hey, all right," Joseph says. He switches it on and shines it at her feet. "Thanks."

Joseph figures she's smiling there in the dark, under her helmet, but he wishes he could know for sure. He'd like to beam the flashlight in her face to find out.

"Be safe," Joseph calls after her as she remounts the trike. When the vehicle pulls away, she gives Joseph a little two-fingered salute. Peace. Victory.

Joseph listens to the fading drone of the ATC as he spotlights his surroundings. Almost immediately the beam falls onto the hair band the woman dropped. She was right about trading up. Simple brown elastic. The scrunchie Joseph gave her was peach-colored and velvety. Not to mention it smelled like Chloe's apple-scented spray-in conditioner and detangler. This brown one the woman lost doesn't smell like anything. It smells like snow.

It was after the accident last month that Joseph started carrying an extra hair band for Chloe on dance school evenings. "If you let her pin her hair up herself, it'll come loose before you get there," Nan had warned Joseph from the bedroom between coughing fits. Her voice was an octave lower than usual that night. Day three of the flu. Not any better, not any worse. "Just put it in a scrunchie," she advised.

"She's almost got it. She's doing great," Joseph had answered from the bathroom where he was watching Chloe work. The kid's concentration was impressive. After carefully placing the last pin, she smiled and gave him a thumbs-up in the mirror. "No sweat," she said to him, and then Joseph echoed her loudly, "No sweat," so Nan could hear.

Of course, Chloe's hair came down in the car just as Nan had predicted. She'd been right and then some. The bun didn't last even two miles.

As Chloe cried to Joseph about her hair at a red light—he was trying to tell her not to worry about it, that maybe someone at the school could help her with her hair, that Miss Linda wouldn't care if she wore her hair down just this once anyway, that the dress and hair codes were more like guidelines rather than hard and fast rules—a Nissan clipped them as it skidded into the ditch. The accident wasn't Joseph's fault—he was sitting still at a red light, trying to talk sense to his daughter, and the driver of the Nissan, a college student, was arguing with her boyfriend via text messages—but because Chloe was already in tears before the accident, it felt to Joseph like his fault somehow. If he'd had a backup scrunchie to toss back to Chloe, if he'd listened to Nan and had his bases covered, he and Chloe still would have been hit by the Nissan, but things wouldn't have seemed as dire. Lesson learned.

As he trudges toward the cemetery, Joseph imagines himself not trudging toward the cemetery, imagines circumstances which wouldn't necessitate his trudging toward the cemetery. If only Miss Linda would've kept her dog at home where pets belong. If only he and Nan would've swapped Brownies and ballet this week. Going back a ways, if only Joseph could've beaten the odds and won the two-against-one argument he had the summer before last with Nan and Chloe about how swim club would be better than dance class. If only. Instead of trudging through snow toward the cemetery, he'd presently be sitting in the warm bleachers at the college's aquatic center, appreciating his daughter's efforts to improve her butterfly, her backstroke.

Arguing for Chloe to become a swimmer, Joseph's mantra had been, "It's a lifetime sport!" but, true or not, this was bad strategy. What does a lifetime have to do with a kid in elementary school? Besides, Nan responded by taking a hardline against pools in general, expressing concerns about plantar warts and waterborne diseases, and when Chloe began to echo her—she pronounced E. coli as "ick-coli"—Joseph knew he'd been defeated. Nan preached the pros of community youth theater for a while—she thought Chloe would be a natural—but when Chloe herself started talking ballet lessons, Nan jumped on board immediately. For Chloe's birthday, Nan brought home Barbie Swan Lake, a three-foot-tall battery-operated doll that dances along with the child. To make Barbie mirror her moves, Chloe had to wear these battery-powered wrist and ankle bracelets. "Like house arrest," Joseph had remarked as he watched Chloe strap on the equipment.

Joseph wonders if it might not be a bad idea to hike back to the car and drive to the cemetery. He thinks there's a bungee cord in his trunk he could use as a leash, and he knows there's a half-bag of honey-roasted cashews in the glove compartment he could use as bait. As much as Joseph hates to admit it, Little Red Riding Hood's mother is right that the dog isn't going to want to come to him. And his phone's in the car. He could call Nan, get some input from her. She's brighter than him in both ways: common sense and book smarts. Talking to her could pay off. It has in the past.

Even as Joseph considers the possibilities of heading back, he continues pushing forward. Willing mind, weak flesh. Or vice versa. At any rate, he has the flashlight, so at least he can see where he's going, and he's come this far. And who knows what the dog's thinking at this point? Out of its element, tired, even scared. Maybe Joseph will remind Clementine of home, and she'll come running, tail wagging, to greet warmly her rescuer. Little Red Riding Hood's mother be damned.

Besides, if Miss Linda or one of the mothers saw Joseph return to the dance school parking lot empty-handed—if he were spotted climbing into his car and then driving away—it would serve only to increase the anxiety and panic he suspects is festering. At this thought, Joseph can't help but worry that the news of Clementine's escape has trickled down to the dancers. To Chloe.

When Joseph steps out of the trees into the cemetery, he stops, listens and calls. It's out of his mouth four or five times before he realizes it. Chloe's name.

"Over here!" When Joseph turns toward the voice, he can make out a group of bodies milling around the mausoleum, thirty or forty yards away. "We got her over here!" A second voice says something more quietly then, and laughter follows. Must be a group of at least four or five. At least one of them's funny.

As Joseph draws close, he's tempted to shine the flashlight on the group, but he's not sure of after-dark graveyard etiquette. When a flashlight beams onto him, though, he returns in kind.

There are six of them, teenagers, all dressed alike in dark hoodies, jeans and ski hats. A couple of them sport backpacks, the kind built for school books, not camping gear. The tallest kid holds Clementine in his arms. Her head is on the boy's shoulder, like she's being burped, and her tail wags rhythmically across his chest like a windshield wiper. When the boy speaks, Clementine's head pops up, and she licks his neck.

"Chloe's her name?" the boy says. "We found her wandering around. We didn't take her."

"I really appreciate it," Joseph says. "Big load off my mind."

"So she's yours then?" the kid says.

"For better or worse," Joseph says, and he moves toward the kid with his hands out. In response, Clementine whips her head around, bares her teeth, snaps her jaws in the air.

The kid turns Clementine away from Joseph, strokes her behind her ears, shushes her.

"You two don't seem to be great friends," one of the other kids says. His hands grip the shoulder straps of his backpack. Joseph is put in mind of a parachutist.

"No," Joseph says. "But I need to get her back to her owner."

"So she's not yours," says the kid holding Clementine. "When I asked, you said she was."

"I meant she's the dog I've been looking for," Joseph says.

"You said 'For better or worse,'" the second kid says.

"Clementine belongs to the owner of the dance school up the road. The En Pointe Academy. My daughter takes classes there. The dog got out by accident, and now I'm fetching her."

"You said her name was Chloe," the kid holding Clementine says.

"My mistake," Joseph says. "Her name's Clementine."

None of the kids responds right away, but they're all intent on Joseph now. Joseph figures them for ninth- or tenth-graders. They're trying to act older and tougher than that, though. Living in a college town, high schoolers looking for trouble are forced to up the ante.

"My name's Derek," the kid holding Clementine says, and then he stops. During the pause, a couple of the other kids smile nervously. One brings the crook of his arm up to his face so he can laugh into it. "Me and my boys will deliver Miss Chloe Clementine to the dance school ourselves," the kid continues. "She seems a little reluctant to go with you. Our car's just past the main gate. We'll run her right over."

The kid laughing into his arm snorts and coughs. The kid standing next to him punches him solidly in the shoulder.

"I'd rather you give her to me," Joseph says. "I don't want to inconvenience you. What are you guys up to, anyway? What's with the outfits and the backpacks?"

"We'd tell you, but then we'd have to…you know," one of the kids says.

This seems to make Derek nervous. "Shut up, Robby," he says, and then he addresses Joseph. "We're just screwing around. Getting into the Halloween spirit."

"Halloween's tomorrow," Joseph says. He and Nan and Chloe plan on clearing out of town like they do every Halloween. The college kids have ruined the holiday for the rest of the town. They get drunk, parade around downtown, fight with one another, bust up the bars, park on people's lawns. Joseph and Nan drive Chloe across the river to Williamstown, West Virginia, so she can get her trick-or-treating in.

"Tonight's Devil's Night," Derek says. "You know, smashing pumpkins, egging houses, soaping windows."

"Drive-by shootings, organ harvestings, virgin sacrifices," Robby says, and there's an explosion of laughter from the group.

"Would you shut the hell up, Robby?" Derek says, but he's laughing now, too. "Look, man," he says, turning to Joseph, "we'll go drop off the dog right now. I think I know the lady. Laura, right?"

"Linda," Joseph says. "Miss Linda."

"I miss her, too," Robby says, and there's more laughter. A crowd won over.

"Seriously, though," Derek says. "I know where you're talking about. My stepmom took a class there last year. We'll have to meet you there, though. Our car's full. You have one?"

"No," Joseph says. "No car." Rock and a hard place. He drums the flashlight against his thigh for a moment. "I'll have to hoof it, I guess. You'll take her directly to the school, right?"

"I could've taught your stepmom how to dance, D," Robby says. "All she had to do was say pretty please."

"You and me are going to have a problem tonight, aren't we?" Derek answers. When he wheels around, Clementine yelps.

"I'm trusting you guys," Joseph says.

He walks with the group as far as the main gate. He beams the flashlight on Clementine as she hops in the front seat to ride shotgun on Derek's lap, and then he watches the car kick up gravel as it pulls onto the road. A couple hands hang out the windows. One's giving Joseph the thumbs-up. Another's flipping him the bird. A house divided.

Joseph follows the car, takes to the shoulder of the road. He's pretty sure that, as the crow flies, taking the road will make for a longer trip than would retracing his steps through the woods and field, but the road's public property, easier walking, and better lit. He doesn't even need the flashlight.

Joseph's trying to stay out of the slop, so he's not over onto the shoulder as far as he should be. That's on him, the pedestrian. But still. The driver of the salt spreader makes no effort to swing around Joseph. He doesn't even slow down. In fact, Joseph thinks he hears the truck accelerate a bit as it passes him, forcing him off the pavement and showering him head to toe with road spray. Snow and ice. Salt and cinders. In his hair, in his eyes. His pants and jacket both. Soaked through.

Joseph knows it's even worse than it looks, even worse than it feels. Helping Chloe with her report on fly ash, he learned that one way they get rid of the stuff is to use it as road deicer. Neither he nor Nan could believe it. You have toxic material on your hands, stuff you need to get rid of because it makes breathing dangerous, so what do you do? You decide to mix it with salt and dump it all over the ground. So what does this make you? This is what Nan wanted to know. Thanks to you, now the stuff's not only in the air, it's in the groundwater. So what are you? Are you stupid? Like you don't know what you're doing? Like you haven't thought it through? Or are you evil? You know exactly what you're doing. You know the ins and outs, the dangerous consequences and repercussions, but you do it anyway.

"Evil?" Joseph had said after listening to Nan. "Irresponsible, no question. Shortsighted, sure. But evil? Evil might be going too far." That was then, though. Ask him now. Now that he's covered in the mess. Muddied and muddled on the dark roadside. Chilled and empty-handed. Ask Joseph now if evil's going too far. Ask him on Devil's Night.

Back at the dance school, before going around to the door, Joseph stops on the sidewalk in front of the picture window. Chloe is framed perfectly in the center. If the scene were a painting or a photograph, she'd qualify as subject.

The Escalade behind Joseph toots its horn. The driver wants Joseph to move because he's blocking her view, or she wants to have a word with him about Clementine, or she wants to congratulate him on his costume. Joseph turns to face the vehicle and takes the flashlight out of his dirty jacket pocket. He switches it on, rests it under his chin, opens his eyes wide and works up a ghoulish snarl. Almost scares himself.

When Joseph turns back to the window, he sees that Chloe's waiting in line to do something. Her cat ears are gone, and her hair, her mane, has come out of its bun. It looks wet, like she's been hiking along with him in the snow for the past hour. Joseph notices a few of the girls have wet heads. Bobbing for apples? Do people still do that? Joseph slips his hand into his damp pocket and finds the hair band he traded down for. He traces the circle of it with his finger.

One girl at a time across the studio floor and then back again. Prancing and skipping and leaping practice. Joseph can't tell these three activities apart, but Chloe says they're different. In front of Chloe in line, two girls bounce in place and hug each other's arms. The girl behind Chloe tugs on Chloe's tail, trying to get a reaction. Chloe, though, doesn't bite. She looks preoccupied. She stands flat-footed and chews her claws with her side teeth. Joseph feels the urge to swat her fingers. You can't nail-chew while working on your butterfly or backstroke. You do, you'll sink.

In last month's car accident, Chloe had lost one of her teeth. It had been on its way out already. She was probably fiddling with it when they were rear-ended. She couldn't leave it alone. "Look how loose," she'd say to Joseph every night at bedtime, wiggling it, and then he'd say, "Want me to take care of it?" and he'd raise a fist. "One in the kisser." She'd laugh and squeal, pull the covers over her head.

The car had been OK to drive post-accident, and after her initial alarm, Chloe was fine at first, even energized and cheered by the adventure. When they arrived at the dance school, though, in the time it took Joseph to undo his seatbelt, climb out of the car, and circle back to her door, Chloe's mood had shifted. She'd remembered her hair problem, discovered blood on her leotard, and realized she'd lost the tooth. Not just lost it, but lost it. Feared gone for good. As in no tooth fairy. And Mom wouldn't get to see.

Joseph eventually talked her down. Kneeling before her there in the parking lot, he'd convinced her Miss Linda wouldn't mind this one time about her hair, that the blood didn't really show on her black leotard, and he promised if she pulled herself together and went inside for class, he'd find the tooth. He wouldn't stop looking until he found it. As Joseph and Chloe negotiated, other dancers and parents walked by, saw the blood and tears, heard the desperation. This guy. Accidents follow him around.

That night, though, had ended happily. Once Joseph got Chloe calmed down and in the school, the tooth was easy to find. Practically found itself. Wedged under the girl's seatbelt. One of the first places Joseph looked.

Just as Joseph is noticing that Miss Linda's not in the studio, she and Little Red Riding Hood's mother come around the corner of the building. Little Red Riding Hood's mother is first. Miss Linda lags behind in her ballet shoes, stepping carefully into Little Red Riding Hood's mother's moon boot prints.

"Well?" Little Red Riding Hood's mother says. "Did you find her?"

"Derek hasn't been here yet?" Joseph says.

"Who?" Miss Linda asks.

"These kids. They found her and were driving her over. I didn't have a leash."

"Who's Derek?" Miss Linda asks.

"His mom took a class from you last year," Joseph says.

"We don't have adult classes," Miss Linda says.

"Why are you all dirty?" Little Red Riding Hood's mother says to Joseph. "You're a mess."

Joseph shakes his head. "They assured me they'd be right over. They were on their way."

Little Red Riding Hood's mother takes her phone out of her sweatshirt pocket and starts to dial. "Where were these kids?" she asks Joseph. "Where did they have Clementine?" She turns to Miss Linda. "Tonight's Devil's Night," she says. "My son wanted to go out, but I put the kibosh on it."

"The cemetery," Joseph says.

"The cemetery?" Miss Linda says, turning to Joseph. There's fresh worry on her face. "What's Devil's Night?"

Joseph opens his mouth to answer, but cat's got his tongue. In the window over Miss Linda's shoulder. Gliding across the studio and then tripping over her own feet and then laughing on the floor. Ashes, ashes. Smooth as spilled milk. A panther or a lynx or a jaguar.

PER LEAGUE RULES

Ten minutes prior to game time, Dom hits fungoes to the Tornados. He stations Morgan, his tall lefty, at first base, and keeps Lenora, adorned in shin guards, next to him at home plate. The rest of the girls line up behind third and then one at a time drift to shortstop to take their warm-ups. For the twelve-year-old rookies, Dom serves easy pop-ups or slow, chest-high bouncers, cherry hops, they can field standing still. The veterans, the thirteen- and fourteen-year-olds, get tougher chances: high flies that twist into the sun and drive them back onto the outfield grass or sharply hit worm-burners deep into the hole. After the girls field the ball, they throw across the diamond to Morgan, and Morgan throws home to Lenora, and Lenora tosses back to Dom.

Dom gets through the line of Tornados twice before the umpire, a high school girl just a few years older than his players, tells him it's time, and then he orders his team to the visitors' dugout, where he'll announce the lineup and deliver his pep talk. Usually Dom's side-by-side at this point with his wife, Natalie, who keeps the scorebook, but tonight her motherly instincts kept her home with Kat, Natalie and Dom's brooding daughter and the Tornados' best player, who's currently giving her father the silent treatment—going on three weeks now—and serving a league-mandated one-game suspension. The silent treatment is a result of the punishment Dom handed down after catching Kat in the house alone with her boy-friend, and the one-game suspension is a result of the tantrum she threw in Saturday evening's season opener. Girl's been busy.

In addition to his wife and daughter, Dom's usual first base coach and Lenora's stepdad, J.R., is a no-show tonight, working a double-shift at Erie Coal and Coke, trying to get in as many hours as possible before the courts decide on the emissions lawsuits. Even if the plant lucks out in state court, there's now a federal case against them, too. At any rate, there's a good chance of layoffs on the horizon. Maybe even a court-mandated shutdown of the whole operation. Then, of course, there's the domino effect: if the coke plant shuts down, mills and foundries all over the region suffer. Dom, like everyone else he knows, is torn. On the one hand, jobs. On the other hand, cancer in the air, in the water.

Kat came home from school one day and told Dom and Natalie that she and some classmates had solved the problem during a group activity in civics class. Employees at the plant should refuse to work until management fixes the problems. In the meantime, the rest of the city should pitch in to take care of these workers and their families, who, Kat maintained, should and would be considered heroes. The activity was worth ten points. The teacher told Kat's group that they'd earned only seven—a low 'C'—because their plan lacked details and real-world feasibility. "Which isn't fair at all," Kat told Dom and Natalie. "This huge problem, and she give us, like, twenty minutes. Real-world feasibility my butt."

Dom can see the coke plant's smokestacks from the ball field. During some evening practices this spring, the breeze coming off the lake would shape the rising smoke into something like a funnel, a white ghost of a tornado—you could allow yourself to see it like this—and Dom would point it out to his squad of Tornados as a good omen. Tonight, though, the smoke hangs flat and gray over the horizon like a dirty blanket, like winter, and watching it makes Dom feel hungover.

There are parents at this evening's game who could step up to offer Dom a hand in his time of need—one could coach a base, another could keep the scorebook—and under different circumstances, a few of them might show the initiative. Given the drama that went down at the previous game, though, Dom's not surprised that no one's offering help tonight. The bleachers are safe. Low risk. Low pressure. Were Dom a bleacher parent this evening, he'd probably sit tight, too.

It's not only the adults lying low. Dom's girls are quieter than usual, uncharacteristically serious and alert, and they're hustling, more or less. Most evenings Dom would appreciate seeing his Tornados adopt this pregame mindset, but tonight it feels unhealthy and foreboding. Truth be told, all day he'd been hoping for a rainout—the last report he saw called for an eighty percent chance of thunderstorms—but wouldn't you know it, not a drop in sight. In fact, right now is the clearest it's been all day. Doppler be damned.

This season's version of the Tornados had an opening day roster of fourteen, but only half a week later, on the brink of game number two, Dom's already down to thirteen girls, maybe even twelve, depending on whether Kat's lost to the Tornados for good or just temporarily. Her suspension's only for tonight's game, but as of a couple days ago, her official stance is she's quit the team. Dom received her announcement via text message, and when he arrived home from work, her jersey was folded neatly and sitting on his chair at the dining room table. Girl's got some drama queen in her.

Besides Kat, the Tornados have lost Amanda Pullium. She hadn't been making good enough grades at school, so her parents hired her a tutor for the summer and forced her to choose between softball and soccer. Dom wasn't surprised by Amanda's decision to ditch the Tornados. Before and after practices, she'd show off her skilled feet and knees by juggling a softball like a hacky sack.

Kids these days, boys and girls alike, are soccer crazy. The North Coast Youth Softball Association shrinks every year, is forced to pass the hat at every game and organize two fundraisers a season just to break even, while the city's three soccer leagues thrive. Dom doesn't like soccer, but he knows the score. From the parents' perspective, there's the issue of fitness, and from the kids' perspective, there's the action. Softball involves a lot of standing around and waiting. You play soccer the right way, you never stop moving. This generation of kids, they don't know patience. They have no experience with it. Dom's flesh and blood included. Kat grows grumpy waiting for microwave popcorn. She's never had to deal with a dial-up internet connection, never had to wait for a cassette to rewind. And boys. This Benji of hers. She's barely fourteen for hell's sake. Dom doesn't even want to think about it, which is why he can't stop thinking about it.

Natalie's theory about Kat's quitting the Tornados is that she's trying to provoke Dom. She doesn't think Kat's quitting will stick, but Dom's not so sure. He's also not sure how much blame he should shoulder for Kat's on-field meltdown Saturday, nor is he sure how warranted her anger with him is about the Benji incident. He'd like Natalie's help, her input and counsel—truth be told, he wouldn't mind her taking the lead on all things Kat—and usually Natalie's not shy about making her voice heard, but recently she's been putting her foot down about her umpiring role in Dom and Kat's wrangling. With daughters and dads, Natalie claims, the temptation is to have everything filtered through mom. It happened in her family growing up, and it wasn't healthy, and she's not about to repeat the mistake.

Just this morning in the kitchen, after Kat left for school, her last day as an eighth-grader, Natalie crystallized for Dom what was at stake as she hollowed out a grapefruit half with a salad fork. "You need to find your way to her, or help her find her way to you, because how Kat ends up dealing with men for the rest of her life depends a lot on what she learns from dealing with her dad."

Dom watched Natalie squeeze the shell of her grapefruit over her bowl and then slurp the juice. "No pressure or anything," Dom said.

"Buck up, Pop," Natalie said, wiping her chin with the cuff of her bathrobe. She picked up her fork and pointed it at Dom. "Come this afternoon, Princess Sunshine is officially high school-bound. We're just getting started here."

In the Tornados' first game of the season last Saturday, the Pythons' pitcher, suffering from opening day jitters, walked the bases full in the top of the first. Kat, in the cleanup slot, was overly anxious and swung wildly at the first pitch, a ball over her head. Dom had given her the sign to take a pitch. Straight out insubordination is what it was.

"Come on, Kat!" Dom had yelled from the third base coaching box, and when she looked at him, he took a few steps toward home and jammed his temple with his forefinger. "Think!" he said. "Don't be stupid!" When Kat stepped out of the batter's box and continued to glare at him, Dom mimicked her swing, cartoonishly launching himself off his feet and swatting at the sky as if assaulting a flock of low-flying birds. Dom's performance drew grimaces from the parents in the bleachers, but the girls on both teams tittered, and the squadron of boys hanging out by the refreshment stand behind the third base dugout looked up from their phones to elbow each other and laugh. Among them was Kat's Benji with his four wristbands, sweaty upper lip, neck acne and black-polished fingernails. He wore his gold Pittsburgh Pirates cap slightly off to the side and low over his eyebrows, and the waistband of his jeans hung a good six inches below the waistband of his boxer-briefs. The bike he sat on looked too small for him, like he might've swiped it from a rack at an elementary school, and the silvery flaming letters across the top of the green frame spelled out the words "Mongoose Mischief Mag." Whatever the hell that's supposed to mean. During pre-game warm-ups, Dom had had to shoo away Benji and his friends from the Tornados' dugout. Turns out the kid had just wanted to give Kat a pack of Starbursts he'd bought for her at the refreshment stand, but still. Time and place.

In response to Dom's performance, Kat turned and heaved her bat into the side of the chain-link backstop—two-handed and over her head, like a pissed-off lumberjack—and then stormed off the diamond, headed in the direction of the parking lot. Halfway there she remembered she was still wearing her batting helmet, and when she ripped it off to spike in the grass, her prescription sports glasses flew off. A couple steps later she took out her mouthguard—special-ordered and custom-fit so she could wear it over her retainer—and flicked it to the side like a cigarette butt. Three hundred and fifty bucks scattered in her wake.

Natalie dropped her scorebook and left the dugout to go after her daughter. Dom watched his wife first retrieve Kat's glasses and mouthguard and then jog to catch up to her and grab her arm from behind. Initially Kat tried to shake her off, but Natalie hung on, and eventually Kat allowed herself to be wrestled into a hug. Benji arrived on the scene then. He pedaled up to Natalie and Kat and just stood there, straddling his bike and sliding his wristbands up and down his thin, hairless forearms, not sure what to do. Dom took some satisfaction in the fact that Kat and Natalie both appeared at first to be ignoring the kid, but when Benji rolled himself close enough to reach out and touch Kat's shoulder, Dom saw Kat move her own hand to cover his.

What happened next surprised Dom, and even though he wondered if he didn't have a right to be angry, to resent being abandoned, he couldn't help but feel some relief when Natalie and Kat, instead of returning to the field, continued toward the parking lot, climbed in the car and drove away. Benji pedaled slowly after them, but when he got to the road, he turned north toward the lake, the opposite direction from Kat and Natalie. Dom watched him turn his hat around backwards and, before riding out of sight, blow a large blue bubble into the wind. Punk must've been working at least three chunks of gum.

On the field, the umpire called to Dom and motioned for him to join her and the Pythons' coach at home plate. When Dom reached them, the girl clicked her ball-strike counter nervously as she explained that Kat had to be called out for unsportsmanlike conduct, and because she'd thrown equipment, per league rules, she had to be ejected from this game and suspended for the next.

"That's the right call," Dom said. "What you have to do."

"Another thing, Coach," the ump said. She pocketed her ball-strike counter and did her best to look Dom in the eye. "I need to remind you of the sportsmanship section of the NCSA Rulebook and Coaching Manual. 'The North Coast Softball Association practices a zero-tolerance policy in regard to unsportsmanlike conduct. Actions that demean players, teams, spectators, coaches and/or officials do not reflect the highest ideals of friendly competition and will not be tolerated. Violators of the policy may be removed from games or practices.'" The ump was lean and tall, a girl you could tell was going to grow beautiful with time, and the way she raised her chin when she spoke to Dom made her seem even taller, made Dom even more sure about her bright future. "I'm not going to run you or write you up this time, Coach," the girl said, "but please cool it, OK? Dealing with the girls is one thing, but I'm only pulling fifteen bucks a game here. That's not enough if the grownups aren't going to behave themselves."

"You memorized that whole rule?" Dom said. "Was that word for word?"

"We had to for orientation," the ump said. "The supervisors were no-joke this year. We even had to watch a video."

"You really think I was out of line just now, though? You think I 'demeaned' Kat? I'd call it a teaching moment. She blew off a sign, and on top of that, I was trying to reinforce the point that a hitter has to know her strike zone. That's a crucial fundamental, right?" Dom looked at the Pythons' coach for support—a new guy, new to the league, maybe even new to coaching in general—but the guy responded by raising his wrist and staring at his watch so he wouldn't have to meet Dom's eyes.

"You know what, though?" Dom said, turning back to the ump. "You're right. I stand reminded of the sportsmanship thing. You've handled this very professionally." He shook hands then with both the umpire and the Pythons' coach, and Dom got the feeling from each of them that the moment they spent hand-in-hand with him couldn't end soon enough.

For the rest of the game, Dom wondered if his biggest sin had been one of omission. Mocking Kat was bad enough, but maybe not going to her after she blew her top was worse. Natalie and Benji had chased her down and comforted her. Maybe he should have. He wondered if that was the mistake he'd end up paying most dearly for. To not go after his own daughter. He'd been stunned, though, by how dangerous and wild she looked chucking that bat. Besides, what could he have said at that point to make things better?

When Kat was a toddler, Dom had a go-to method to handle her tantrums. He used to pretend to hurt himself. It distracted her, cracked her up. He'd walk into a wall, trip over his own feet or stick a spoon in his eye to get her to giggle her way out of a funk. The Three Stooges strategy. Natalie had been against the technique at first but eventually relented and even summoned Dom now and then to work his cartoon violence magic when Kat was being especially fussy. Its effectiveness was inarguable. As Kat grew older, Dom's slapstick routines eventually stopped working, of course, but he now wondered if he might be able to wring out a few more years if he upped the ante. He could slam his hand in a car door. Fall off a roof. Buy a gun and shoot himself in the foot. Trim one of his ears with hedge clippers. Lick a light socket. Take a skinny dip with the tumor-ridden shiners and frogs in the mucky sluice at the foot of the coke plant. Whatever it takes. He loves the girl after all.

This evening's opposing pitcher is on the mound and warming up. She's under five feet tall, Dom guesses, which is why he's surprised by the impressive pop of the catcher's mitt. Dom's not sure where the power's coming from. Besides being short, the girl's skin and bones. No hips. No butt. Nothing behind the ball except will and want-to. Dom catches the eye of the Coyotes' head coach across the diamond and nods, raising his eyebrows. He doesn't recognize this girl, doesn't remember her from last year, but there's no denying little sister can sling it.

As Dom waits in the dugout for the Tornados to situate themselves and their gear—sports drinks, sunflower seeds, bubble gum, batting gloves, eye-black, sunglasses, scrunchies—he tries to decide whether or not to address the Kat situation. He'd like it not to be a distraction, but he's not sure how to ensure this: ignore it or get it out in the open. Either way he can imagine making things worse. He can't think of a good way to find out, but it might help him manage the situation if he knew whom the Tornados blamed, Kat or him. He wonders about the discussions the girls had inevitably had with their parents after the last game. He wonders if, in the Tornados' eyes, he's a laughingstock or a villain, a victim of circumstance or a bully. He wonders if they see Kat as a crybaby or a hero. He wonders if it's too late to switch places with J.R. for the night. One poison-belching coke oven for one junior girls softball team. Even up. From the fire to the furnace. And vice versa.

Bottom line is, while Dom knows he shouldn't have embarrassed Kat, it was a matter of not thinking as opposed to malicious intent. Eventually, he'd tell her that. Still, he also knows that under normal circumstances her anger at him would've turned her into a tiger on the field, not a quitter. In the days leading up to the game, it seemed as if she were waiting for him to offend her so she'd have reason to explode. In turn, he'd grown sick of tiptoeing around her, so he realizes his outburst was a kind of release, too. He'd let it out, and then she'd let it out.

Two weeks before the season opener, Dom had come home early from work one afternoon to find Kat making out with Benji. The boy was seated in the chair at the head of the dining room table, the chair Dom usually sat in, and Kat was in his lap, straddling him. They both had all their clothes on, and their hands were in plain sight, stroking each other's hair, and they were downstairs in the dining room rather than upstairs in Kat's bedroom, so it could've been worse. This is what Natalie told Dom later. She wanted Dom to balance his anger with some appreciation of the relative innocence and self-control the kids had demonstrated. "They were probably alone in the house for more than an hour," Natalie told Dom when he came to bed that night.

"Their retainers were side-by-side on the table," Dom said. "The table we eat on. They were touching. Kat's retainer was touching this Benji kid's retainer."

"I'm telling you," Natalie said, "if after more than an hour they got no further than kissing in the dining room, we should take that as a good sign."

"Good sign?" Dom said. "'Keep Out.' That's a good sign. 'No Trespassing.' 'Private Property.'"

When Dom had walked in on Kat and Benji, the first thing he'd done was whirl around, turn his back to them out of equal parts anger and embarrassment. "Bye, Benji!" he bellowed.

Dom didn't turn to face Kat until he heard the back door slam—the kid must've stowed his bike on the rear patio so it would be out of sight—and then he stared at her red, silent face for a long, dumbfounded moment before informing her she was grounded for a month.

"A month? For kissing my boyfriend?" she said.

"For having him here without Mom or me home," Dom answered. "Don't play dumb."

"That rule's dumb," Kat said. "I'm going to be in high school."

"Go to your room," Dom said. "I don't want to look at you right now. And no phone. No texting. No emailing. No Facebooking."

"Fine."

"You're off the grid. Got it?"

"What you're saying, yes. Why you're being such a jerk-tyrant, no."

Since then, when it comes to Dom, Kat's been mute. Even after Natalie, playing negotiator, eased the grounding back from a month to two weeks and clarified that Kat wouldn't have to turn down any babysitting gigs, Kat still wouldn't talk to him. The way Dom saw it, she'd twisted things in her mind on purpose so she could stay mad. Kat told Natalie that, as far as she was concerned, she'd been grounded because Dom didn't want her to have boyfriends and because he especially hated Benji.

"That's not true," Dom told Natalie when she told him what Kat had said. "Did you tell her that's not true?"

"I told her you don't even really know Benji, so it wouldn't make any sense for you to have it in for him. When she brought up how you made fun of the way he threw when he and Kat were playing catch in the backyard last week, and how you mocked the size of his bike, and how you cracked wise when she told you he was in the gifted program at school, I told her you have never said anything to me about not wanting her to have boyfriends." Natalie paused. "Truth is, though, I wonder if the girl's onto you a bit."

"Did I tell you she called me a tyrant?" Dom said. "Where'd she pick that up? Does she know what a tyrant is? A real tyrant?"

"Vocabulary," Natalie said, "is not the issue here."

Dom had thought game day might bring Kat around. He'd asked Natalie to suggest to Kat that the team could use her at the Coyotes game to cheer them on, and he'd called the league chair for clarification to make sure Kat was allowed to sit in the dugout with her teammates despite the suspension, but when he left for the field this evening, Natalie and Kat were both in sweats, sitting on the couch, watching a cake building contest on one of the food channels. The contestants were done baking and decorating, so all that was left for them to do was move their cakes from the kitchen to the display stage for judging. The cakes were huge, complicated and fragile, so tension was high. The camera focused on a fat, bald baker who seemed to be bearing most of the weight of his team's creation, a *Star Wars*-themed wedding cake. R2D2 and C3PO in tuxes. A misshapen Chewbacca appeared to be either priest or ring bearer.

As the camera zoomed in for a close-up of the sweat beads forming on the fat baker's bald head, one of his assistants slipped, and the cake started to slide, and the baker overcompensated. The cake hit the floor. And then the cake hit the floor again in slow motion. And then again. And then once more. Same cake, same floor. Like the show wanted its viewers wallowing in this cake's destruction. Like there was a point to be made.

Dom stood behind the couch and chuckled. "Ouch," he said.

Natalie pulled a throw pillow to her chest and groaned. "A caketastrophe," she said.

"Wouldn't have won anyway," Kat said. On TV, the baker buried his head in his hands, and his shoulders shook. Kat turned toward Natalie to make clear she was addressing only her mother. "His team's cake was the worst one. It sucked. That's what he should be crying about."

"Still," Natalie said. "All that work."

"Cry me a river," Kat said. "Let's have a pity party."

Dom watched the screen as one of the other competitors went over to the weeping baker and wrapped an arm around his shoulder. "That right there," Dom said. "Graciousness. Goodwill. What the confectionary arts are all about."

"Can we see what else is on, Mom?" Kat grabbed the remote before Natalie could answer.

"I'm off," Dom said. "Wish us luck."

"TV's so lame," Kat said as she zoomed through the channels. "Remember when it used to be good?"

Lined up in front of Dom on the dugout bench, the Tornados are all ears. He can tell the girls need something from him—they can see the darts being fired by the Coyotes' pitcher, can hear the stinging retort of the Coyotes' catcher's mitt as well as he can—but his mind's a blank slate. The only thing he can think to do is read the lineup and watch his leadoff hitter, Hayley Pierce, put on a helmet and drag a bat to the on-deck circle. A lamb to the slaughter. A canary down the mine shaft, down the toxic smokestack. If only Dom had handy a blindfold and cigarette, he could properly equip the poor girl.

Dom's about halfway across the field to the third base coaching box when he pulls a U-turn and sprints back to the Tornados' dugout. He grabs the chain-link screen with his fingers, shakes it like he's on the wrong side of a cage and screams, "Who are we?" and the girls answer, "Tornados!" and then he asks them again and receives the same answer, but this time it's louder and more unified, and then Dom asks, "What do Tornados do?" and the girls scream back, "Win!" and then he tells them, "I can't hear you!" and then they scream "Win!" even more loudly, and then they all clap and fist-bump and hug, like they're sharing newly received good news, the exact good news they'd been waiting to hear.

On his jog back across the diamond, Dom grins and nods at the Coyote pitcher as he passes behind the rubber, and she smiles widely back at him, like he's told her a joke, and then she cranes her neck, points her lip-glossed lips to the patchy sky and howls, and her infielders answer her in kind, and then her outfielders, and then her bench, and Dom's surrounded.

Four innings into the game, the rout's in full swing. The Tornados can't touch Ray-Ray—that's the name the Coyote players and fans scream whenever the diminutive assassin strikes out another Tornado—and Dom's pitcher, twelve-year-old Caitlin Pietre, is going through some growing pains. This experience will help her down the road, toughen her up, but that's cold comfort tonight. Dom had worried this would happen, but he'd had no choice. With Kat and Amanda gone, Caitlin's the only pitcher he's got. His thinking going into the season was to bring Caitlin along slowly, give her a well chosen inning here and there to gain some confidence and thereby develop an arm the Tornados could count on for next year. That was Plan A. Plan B, it turns out, is more painful. Even though the game is four innings old, Caitlin's managed to retire only three hitters. The Coyotes scored ten in the first, so the mercy rule has kicked in. Now the Coyotes are allowed to score only one run per inning until the Tornados can cut the lead to single digits.

Dom takes Caitlin aside before the bottom of the fourth to tell her he admires her, respects how she keeps taking the ball and heading back out there.

"I keep taking it because you keep giving it to me, and you keep giving it to me because there's nobody else," Caitlin says, her voice breaking a little, and then she shuffles off to the rubber to tee up a few more peaches for the Coyotes.

A half-inning later, Morgan, who's on deck, sticks her head into the dugout. "Kat's here, Coach," she says.

Dom walks around to the fence to see his daughter approaching from the parking lot, riding on the back of Benji's bike. When the bike hits the grass, Kat jumps off and walks to the field. She comes through the fence, passes right by Dom, and takes a seat in the dugout. She's not wearing her Tornados jersey, but she's wearing her cap. She asks her teammates what the score is and then yells to Morgan at the plate, "Little knock, M-Dog! Little knock to get us started!" Not even a glance in Dom's direction.

What Dom wants to do is call Kat out of the dugout, draw her close and whisper the right thing into her ear. "Sorry" or "Love you" or "Let's not be afraid of each other" or "Please grow up to be like your mother" or "Please erase from your mind all the mistakes I've made, and let me start over" or "You are already better at softball than I have ever been at anything." What he does instead is walk down the third base line, lean over the fence and summon Benji. The kid approaches Dom on foot, leaves his bike behind with his buddies at the snack bar.

"Her riding on the back of your bike like that is dangerous," Dom says to the kid when he's within range. "Don't do that anymore. Not with Kat."

"Right," Benji says. The kid's trying his damndest to grow a moustache, and he strokes his stubble nervously with his thumb. Today his nails are painted white-black-white-black, every other finger, like piano keys. "It was just a few seconds on the parking lot," Benji says, drawing closer. "On the road we walked."

"Don't do it even for just a few seconds," Dom says. "Don't do it with anyone's daughter."

Benji smirks nervously and looks over Dom's shoulder toward the field. "Right," he says.

"Does Kat's mom knows she's here with you?"

Benji nods. "She said it was OK. It was her idea. Kat has to ride home with you, though." The kid brings his fist to his chin and cracks his knuckles. "That's what her mom said."

Without forethought Dom reaches his hand over the fence and palms Benji's bony shoulder. And he squeezes. He squeezes a little harder than he wants to. "Whether her mom said it or not," Dom says, "that's what's happening."

Benji steps back from the fence, slips Dom's hand. There's sheepish fear in the kid's eyes, but Dom sees anger there, too. "Right," the kid says, and he levels his eyes with Dom's, and Dom knows the kid hates him. Benji's on his way back to the snack bar and his friends and his bike before Dom can get another word in.

Anger hadn't been a goal of Dom's. Hate hadn't been a goal. In some ways, talking to Benji didn't feel all that different from talking to Kat. That same fine line. Every word Dom said felt wrong. Every word said back to him sounded wrong. This Benji must have parents. Adults he has to answer to. Dom wonders if he'd have their support in how he'd just tried to deal with their son. It takes a village, they might say appreciatively. Or would they tell Dom to cool it? You raise your kid, we'll raise ours. You want to lose your hand, touch our son again.

Dom didn't hurt Benji. He just squeezed a shoulder to get the kid's attention. Like you do with an overly excited pet. A dog by the scruff of the neck or by the muzzle. So the kid would understand Dom was for real. So the kid would focus. To wipe the smirk off the kid's face so he could focus. Something like patting the kid's shoulder or sticking out his hand to invite Benji to shake, though, probably would've been better. Better real-world feasibility. Or maybe Dom should've just stuck his hands in his pockets and forgot he had them. Like a soccer player would. At any rate, hindsight's 20-20. Or it's not. Not even hindsight is.

The rain seems to hit everyone else before it hits Dom. Umbrellas bloom in the bleachers as fans scurry to the parking lot, and the Coyotes and Tornados aren't far behind. "Game's called. There's lightning out there," the ump says to Dom as she flees, and when Dom turns to face the outfield, he sees bolts zigzagging the sky over the lake. They could be shooting from the coke plant's smokestacks. You could allow yourself to see the scene like this.

Inside the plant, J.R., almost halfway through his second shift, probably doesn't even know it's raining. The noise, the heat. If he does know, it makes no difference. Rain or shine, rain or acid rain, his livelihood hangs in the balance.

J.R. told Dom that you can make iron without coke these days—the technology has existed for a while—but even though the process is cleaner and uses less energy, the industry's been slow to move. There's the up-front expense and effort. New equipment. New training. The willingness required to think outside the box. In J.R.'s opinion, the bigwigs at Erie Coal and Coke would rather go under because, in the short term, going under is cheaper and easier.

"Egos and checkbooks," Dom had said.

"And the world goes round," J.R. had said.

When the hail starts, Dom ducks into the dugout to gather the team's equipment and pick up after his Tornados. Helmets, bats, catcher's gear. Gum wrappers, plastic bottles. A stray wristband. A warm-up jacket. Add equipment manager to Dom's job description. Add custodian. Add lost-and-found. Man doesn't have enough hands. And the ones he does have can't always be trusted. Nothing to cry about. Nothing to throw a pity party over. Just the way things are.

Dom's not worried about Kat. He'd left the driver side window halfway down, so she shouldn't have any problem letting herself in. She's probably wondering what's keeping him, though, as she watches the rain and then hail and then rain again bounce off the windshield.

Could be Benji's in the car with Kat. She would've offered him a ride home. This isn't Mongoose weather. The kid might have it on his mind to steal a smooch or two in the backseat before Dom shows, but that doesn't necessarily mean Kat's game. Or vice versa. Maybe Benji's the one who's not game. Or maybe he's not in the car with Kat after all. Could be after his exchange with Dom, the kid wouldn't dream of letting Dom drive him home. Could be Benji's pedaling home right now. Doppler be damned. In and out of blurry headlights, dodging potholes and lightning bolts, fighting wind, licking road spray off his beginner's moustache.

Dom doesn't wish the kid ill. He doesn't. He wishes him home safe and sound. Traveling mercies. Godspeed.

Dom drops himself on the middle of the bench, swings his legs up, lies his head back, closes his eyes and listens to the pinging on the dugout roof pick up then slow down then pick up again. Thunder crashes miles away over the lake, and then seconds later another rumbling sounds like it's coming from the south. Like there are two storms. Or one with two heads that's disagreeing with itself. On the one hand, but on the other hand, and Dom's caught in the middle. Like the argument's over him. Like it's none of his business. Either way, he's going to wait this one out.

SAFARI SUPPER

hors d'oeuvres

The hastily assembled spread on the dining room table—Pringles, Wheat Thins, a bottle-and-a-half of Merlot, four cans of Diet Dr. Pepper, a bowl of leftover Halloween candy—might be worse than no spread at all. This is one reason why the hosts, Wendy and Drew Pike-Stuyvesant, are ashamed of and angry with each other. Another reason is that Wendy and Drew had been expecting their guests, the Fabulous 40s and 50s of St. Jude's Episcopal, next Friday, not this Friday. And then, finally, there's this: neither Drew nor Wendy is good in a crisis, and they're both reminded of this personal shortcoming when they see it mirrored in the other. So the nature of the malice between them this evening is, for whatever this is worth, intimate and complex.

Following their cupboard-raiding, table-setting frenzy, Drew and Wendy take pains to avoid each other as they mingle sheepishly among their guests, but the physical distance they keep between them doesn't work to mute the tension, but rather amplifies it, makes a spectacle of it. When Wendy notices from across the room the not one but two missed belt loops on Drew's khakis, she clamps her teeth and pinches her earlobe white, and when Drew spots Wendy's Zoloft and his ten-year-old daughter Dawn's Ritalin sitting where they always sit, in plain sight on top of the hutch, he gasps audibly and breaks toward them with the notion of rushing them into the kitchen. In his hustle, though, he fumbles the bottles, and one rolls under the table, so he's forced to his knees and elbows to retrieve it, and when he's down there Dawn drops to join him, asks loudly, giddily, "What are you freakin' doing down here, Dad?" and when father and daughter stand up at the same time, they bump heads, and Dawn sobs for a moment and then, without transition, giggles herself breathless.

The effect of Drew's rush to stash the pills is, of course, that it turns heads, spotlights the very things he aims to hide. After the fact, this is what Wendy whisper-scolds him about in the kitchen. She has Drew backed up against the microwave, which still holds the bean burritos Dawn and her older brother Andy had been heating up when the doorbell rang twenty minutes ago.

"It's when you hiss at me like this," Drew answers. "It's a wonder I'm not the one on pills." When Wendy takes a step back and rests her folded hands under her chin, Drew apologizes, but there's a "but" attached, as in, "But seriously, how hard is it to mark a date correctly?" He tells her to watch carefully as he takes the pen by the phone, circles today's date on the calendar by the refrigerator—he knows he's being an ass but can't stop himself—and writes "Progressive Dinner" in the empty space.

The calendar's January photograph, captioned with the phrase "Pure Michigan!" depicts a team of thick-tailed, frost-breathing Huskies pulling an unmanned sled cross a sunny tundra-like field, probably somewhere in the Upper Peninsula. Were one of Drew and Wendy's guests to stray into the kitchen at this moment, he or she might at first note the similarities between the setting in the photograph and the setting outside—Chicago is still de-icing from the storm the night before—and then the guest might observe Drew's intense focus on the calendar along with Wendy's wide-eyed exasperation and assume the couple to be arguing about vacation plans or animal cruelty or global warming.

Wendy turns on her heel and retreats to the dining room, so Drew's left alone in the kitchen with the cold burritos, the masterless snow dogs, and the sudden suspicion he's left the TV on in the bedroom. If someone uses the upstairs bathroom, they might hear it, perhaps even take the initiative to wander down the hall to turn it off. Drew doesn't remember what channel he left it on, whether or not it was something respectable. There's a lot of good stuff in the Platinum Package, but a lot of crap, too. Stuff you watch only with the mute button on or the house empty. This crap, you don't necessarily set out to watch it, but it gets watched.

Wendy hates Drew watching TV alone in the bedroom. She often uses the word "sequester" when she complains about it. Drew originally thought she was using the word incorrectly, didn't think "sequestering" was something one could do to oneself, but then he looked it up and realized her usage was fine. Because he never told her he'd suspected she was wrong, though, there was no need to admit anything. Drew has had more than a few arguments like this with Wendy, arguments she's unaware that she's had, that she's won.

It was almost a year ago that the couple, both very aware, had a big blow up about Drew's sequestering. It was at least peripherally about this. After church one Sunday, Wendy had been talking to a guy who's since moved away, a single guy, Patrick something, and Drew heard her say, "Thanks, but I don't think so. I don't golf. Drew used to, but now he just sequesters himself in the bedroom on Saturdays to watch TV." Wendy said it loudly so Drew would hear. She meant it funny, she told him later. Couples tease each other in public. It's like flirting for married people. But Drew didn't think it was funny, and he didn't think this Patrick's follow-up line about TV being a married man's best friend was funny either, and he couldn't help but be irritated that this Patrick had invited his wife to play golf.

In response, Drew had walked out of the sanctuary, proceeded to the fellowship hall to rustle up the kids, and then headed out to the car with them to wait for Wendy. When she got there, she was angry. She said he'd embarrassed her, the way he'd stormed off. Drew was incredulous. He'd embarrassed her? The spat lasted a couple weeks, off and on. Over the course of their marriage, it's the only full-fledged fight Drew remembers that didn't end in an apology session. Neither of them ever said sorry. To this day. The matter simply lost steam, faded.

When Drew pushes himself away from the counter, he notices the blinking microwave timer. When he pops open the door, he comes face-to-face with the pair of burritos. An ugly sight. The kids over-nuke everything. It takes four bites for him to down the first, and he devours the second in two. As he eats, he becomes more convinced that he left the TV on upstairs—by the time he's finished chewing and wiping his mouth on the dishtowel by the sink, he's positive of it—but he still can't remember for the life of him what he was watching. The more he strains to remember, the more worried he becomes. He needs to get up there. Pronto.

With their hosts battling in the kitchen, the guests have been desperate for something else to focus on, so they've gamely engaged twelve-year-old Andy, who's suddenly sporting a red cape over his Blackhawks jersey and performing under-practiced magic tricks in the living room. After each botched attempt, Dawn, Andy's anti-assistant, provides detailed and thunderous commentary on how her brother's trick went awry, and when Andy finally succeeds in pulling one off—the disappearance and then re-appearance of a quarter—Dawn announces the secret behind the illusion. "There are two freakin' coins! Check the freakin' dates!" Like she's performed her own trick by swallowing a microphone.

"Can you turn water into wine, Houdini?" Jerry Stepnoski smiles at Andy and then at everyone else in the room as he pours the last few drips of Merlot into his wife Karen's glass. "Maybe a nice freakin' Beaujolais?"

Wendy emerges from the kitchen too late to hear the line but in time to see everyone grinning, so she grins, too. She tries to keep this grin even as Drew re-enters into the room, winds his way through the guests without as much as an "excuse me," and ascends the stairs quickly, heavily, two-at-a-time.

"Where you goin', Dad?" Dawn bellows. When there's no response, she flies up the stairs after him, serving as her own booming echo. "Hey, Dad! Where's the freakin' fire?"

soup

On the drive from the Pike-Stuyvesants' to the Markhams', from Hyde Park to Bucktown, Brangwynne Koonce, President of the Fabulous 40s and 50s, wonders how the night could've started worse. Technically speaking, Drew and Wendy shouldn't even be in FFF. Wendy shouldn't, anyway. She's only thirty-eight. Does Brangwynne need to go to the extreme of checking drivers' licenses? Requiring birth certificates? Someone like Wendy could use another couple years to mature. She had the easiest course of the night and couldn't pull it off. You volunteer to do something for a group you shouldn't even officially be a part of, the least you can do is remember. The woman had to get off her elliptical trainer to answer the door for pete's sake. She greeted her guests in lycra shorts and a sweaty sports bra, a tiny music player clipped to her shoulder strap, earphones in her head. Embarrassing for everyone. Bad enough. But then not to own up to the fact that she'd forgotten, to try to cover up and muddle through. That's when embarrassing became insulting. And the husband storming around like a moody toddler. The clownish children. That dreadful word the girl kept screaming. Freakin'. The least Wendy could've done for her neglected guests was kennel the children in their rooms.

At any rate, what's done is done. There are still three courses to go, and Brangwynne is heartened by her faith in the upcoming soup course. Peter and Ginger Markham are both wizards in the kitchen—their cream of butternut squash might just be what's needed to get the evening back on track—and their children are of the grown and moved out variety. Brangwynne's spirits lift when she sees the couple on their front steps, waving to their arriving guests. Six cars, eleven diners. Five couples and Brangwynne.

When Brangwynne founded FFF a year ago, she knew the make-up of the group would be mostly couples, but she'd hoped it might attract a few singles, too. Patrick Bogardus, especially. He wore great sweaters, and his singing voice, a rich tenor, resonated with Brangwynne, echoed in her ears long after the service was over. He'd attended the late service on Sundays—*Meet the Press* ran during the early liturgy, he told her once, and he was a fan from way back—so she began attending the late service, too, even though she'd always been an early riser. She'd never been able to stay in bed past six-thirty, so sleeping in wasn't an option. For a couple Sundays in a row she tried to watch *Meet the Press*, but it made her feel tense and nervous, so more often than not she ended up attending both Sunday services at St. Jude's. Back-to-back. No one, not even Father Garrett, seemed to notice.

Brangwynne would try to sit in the pew in front of Patrick so she could listen. She wished everyone else in the sanctuary, choir included, would be struck mute—a miracle in reverse—so she could experience his voice more directly and clearly. When the congregation exchanged the peace and Patrick would turn to her, she'd be moved by his puffy red eyes, amazed by how deeply the liturgy affected him, and she loved how he used both hands on her in greeting. He'd take her right in his right, but where his left ended up varied. Her shoulder, her forearm. He once reached around and rested it lightly on her back as if asking her to dance. Another time, when she'd worn new earrings, he used two fingers to brush her earlobe as he complimented her on them, and when she rose a few moments later to go to the altar for the bread and wine—her second helping of the day—she discovered she was shivering.

Ginger Markham and her beaded moccasins. Peter Markham and his full, curly beard. Their spotless home's wood-stove warmth. Brangwynne prefers most couples individually, one at a time—they're more digestible that way—but Peter and Ginger she likes as a set. When she walks through their door, she likes how Peter's large, heavy hands helping her off with her coat complement the lightness of Ginger's lips on her cheek. Brangwynne doesn't often entertain thoughts of marriage anymore, but here, under the affectionate care of the Markhams, she thinks for a moment she could see herself married to them. Not like bigamy. Not like Peter would have two wives. He'd have Ginger, and then he and Ginger as a couple would have a wife, Brangwynne, and she wouldn't have a husband and a wife, she'd have a couple. Where two or three are gathered together. Brangwynne surprises herself with this notion, is surprised by the tingling in her stomach as Peter and Ginger, one on either side, escort her into the dining room to get her approval on their beautiful table settings. She sniffs the air. Cumin and cinnamon. A touch of nutmeg. Perfect.

When Ginger and Peter ask Brangwynne how it went at the Pike-Stuyvesants, why Drew and Wendy didn't continue on with the rest of the group, Brangwynne just raises her eyebrows and shakes her head, and the three of them exchange small, sympathetic smiles.

Peter and Ginger tell their guests to sit wherever they'd like, except for Brangwynne, whom they want with them at the head of the table. There's a small package by Brangwynne's bowl—the bow is larger than the box—and as she opens it, Ginger, to Brangwynne's right, and Peter, to her left, take turns explaining to the other guests how much Brangwynne does for the Fabulous 40s and 50s, how selfless she is in sacrificing her time. By the sounds of it, the gift's more than simply a late Christmas present; it's an award of sorts. Something Brangwynne's earned.

Brangwynne hasn't seen Patrick Bogardus in about a year. Just as she was getting FFF up and running, his job transferred him out of town, so it surprises her now to be thinking of him. She'd like him here, though, to watch her open her gift, a gorgeous starfish brooch made of lake glass. Ginger found all the glass herself, mostly on the beach in Winnetka, and then had an artist friend of hers fashion the brooch. Brangwynne would've liked Patrick to be here to ooh and ahh along with everyone else, and when the moment came for someone to help her pin the starfish on her sweater— overcome with gratitude and pride, her hands are shaking too much to do it herself—she would've liked him to be the one to step up.

As it is, no one moves to pin the brooch on Brangwynne. Several women ask if they can get a closer look, and as it's carefully passed around the table like an infant at a family reunion, a quick but spirited mini-discussion breaks out among the men about whether or not there is such a thing as a freshwater starfish, but when the brooch finally makes its way back to Brangwynne, Peter simply says grace, and then Ginger rises to take the rolls out of the oven.

There are two kinds of rolls: lemon poppy and pumpernickel. A few of the couples take one of each and split them so neither husband nor wife has to miss out on either. Before the basket of rolls reaches Brangwynne, she empties her glass of Chardonnay, excuses herself and heads to the bathroom to use the mirror. She pins and unpins the brooch three times before she's satisfied it's in the right spot.

When she gets back to the table, her glass is filled with Pinot Grigio. Eventually, a nice Riesling comes around.

entree

Kyle's surprised to hear the doorbell. Surprised it was necessary. He figured Sara would've been stationed at the window, on the lookout for her guests. He figured she would've been smiling in the open door before the guests had even climbed out of their cars. Smiling and ready with her story.

This bug, it had hit Kyle out of nowhere. One minute he was in his office trying to finish up emails so he could get home early to help Sara get ready, and the next minute he was doubled over in the corner retching into his wastebasket. Each wave felt like it had to be the last, but it wasn't. When Graber in the next office came over to check on him—"You dying in here?"—Kyle was drenched in sweat, half delirious.

He recovered enough to make his way to the parking garage and drive himself home, but he probably shouldn't have. Just after he let himself into the house, he had a second bout of intestinal violence in the downstairs bathroom. This was three hours ago. He thinks he's through the worst of it now, but he still feels weak, his ribs and back throb, and he looks like he popped off to the wrong guy. There are purple patches of broken blood vessels under both eyes. In the aftermath of his outburst in the downstairs bathroom, Sara had told him, not for the first time, that he was a melodramatic vomiter.

After helping him into bed and cleaning up after him, Sara announced her intentions to go ahead with the dinner—what else is she supposed to do with eighteen dressed Cornish hens?—and, furthermore, rather than tell the guests that Kyle's upstairs in bed with the stomach flu, she's going to tell them that he got hung up at work, that something unforeseen and unavoidable had come up. "It's not a one hundred percent lie," Sara said. "You were at work, and it was unforeseen and unavoidable."

An hour before the guests' scheduled arrival, Sara parked Kyle's car at the dentist's office a block away, and she's stowed his jacket and briefcase in the bedroom closet. She's resolved to keep everyone downstairs by announcing that the only available bathroom is the tiny one off the study. The upstairs facility is, alas, out of order. Again, the way she figures it, it's not a full-blown lie she's telling, considering how the handle of the upstairs toilet has to be jiggled and how the sink spigot drips unless the hot water handle is positioned just so.

When Kyle asked Sara why she simply doesn't tell their guests the truth, she put the shoe on the other foot, said if she were a dinner guest at someone's house and before the meal was told there was a sick person upstairs, she'd be grossed out. It would kill her appetite. She'd immediately start thinking exit strategy.

"So you'd want to be lied to?" Kyle said.

"I'd prefer not knowing," Sara answered. "Besides, I'd like to think my host would have been responsible enough to triple-Lysol everything the ill person touched."

Kyle wondered how one can simultaneously not know something and hope to be protected from it, but he didn't have the energy to pursue the matter. Besides, the least he can do is work with Sara on this. His timing's horrible, and he feels guilty. Not that getting sick is his fault, but it feels like it could be. He'd been half-contemplating the possibility of faking something to get out of this dinner—a migraine or sore throat—so maybe he got what he deserved. Karma. The least he can do is promise Sara he'll stay quiet.

"You won't hear a peep from me," he told her. "I won't even turn on the TV. I'm Anne Frank up here, hiding from Nazis."

"I know you don't like them all, Kyle, but Nazis? Really? They're Episcopalians."

"Nazis in the sense that I'm Anne Frank hiding from them."

"You're sick," Sara had said. "Both kinds."

It's not long after the doorbell rings that Kyle begins to hear the rhythms of friendly conversation, the occasional burst of polite laughter, and then, after ten or fifteen minutes pass, the squeak of dining room chairs and the clinking of silverware and wine glasses. He smells the food—along with the stuffed hens, Sara has roasted asparagus and prepared a baked corn casserole, Kyle's mother's recipe—and he's actually beginning to feel a little hungry. This kind of stomach bug, it's here and then gone. Messes you up something awful but doesn't linger. Kyle's disappointed in himself for thinking this, but if he's honest, he'd have to admit it's not a bad trade-off. A few hours of physical agony in exchange for sitting out the progressive dinner. He's accepted worse deals.

What's Kyle's problem with St. Jude's and the Fabulous 40s and 50s? He and Sara have been down this road. Is it that he finds them boring? If that's all it is, Kyle has to admit it sounds petty. Who does he think he is? What makes him so exciting? Sara would like to get more involved at church, to try to be more social. Volunteering for a leg of the progressive dinner was her first attempt. When she was awarded the main course, she felt affirmed. Kyle understands Sara's desire for a more dynamic social circle, and if it were only the St. Jude's women, he'd have no problem. He finds all of them relatively charming and easy enough to talk to. Harmless. Their husbands, though. It's not that they aren't decent people; it's just that Kyle feels restless around them and, what? Under-prepared? Kyle follows politics, but he focuses on the national level, whereas the St. Jude's crew's interests seem primarily local. And in conversation, they come on like survey takers. After the Fisk and Crawford coal plants shut down, Kyle was approached by a gang of them during coffee hour one Sunday morning and asked how he thought the sites should be redeveloped. His confession that he hadn't given the issue much thought didn't stop the inquisition, though, it just shifted it. As he poured Cremora into his half-full paper cup of weak coffee, he was quizzed about the cost and methods of eliminating the non-disinfected sewage effluent flowing through the city's neighborhoods. The men seemed oddly eager to hear what he had to say, and Kyle got the sense he'd been cast in the role of tiebreaker. When he tried to lighten things up by saying he was pro-clean, anti-dirty, no one laughed. Instead, the topic switched to the impending city teachers' strike and, more broadly, to the questionable legitimacy of public employee unions. Where did his sympathies lie? When one man interrupted to protest the wording of the question, Kyle excused himself and hid out in the men's room until the service started.

It's not just politics, though. It's not just one thing. When conversation shifts away from hot button controversies, the St. Jude's men, the lot of them, become storytellers. Bad, self-interested ones. They take long turns recounting personal experiences, most of which seem to Kyle pointless and anticlimactic. After the Lessons and Carols Christmas service last month, one of the guys—it was either a Gary or a Jerry—had Kyle cornered for twenty minutes as he gave a blow-by-blow account of the patio stairs he'd built that fall. Kyle doesn't have a patio. He doesn't have a toolbox. And the guy with the meticulous beard, Peter Markham, he'll hold forth about his garden as if he were behind a podium. His thought process in choosing what tomato varieties to plant. His latest strategies to foil bugs and rabbits.

When Kyle tried to explain to Sara about the men, she at first missed his point, telling him that this was their way of trying to include him, of trying to make him feel part of things, and she told him she was sure he could think of a good story to share if he put some effort into it. When she finally caught his drift, she tried to undermine Kyle's complaints with humor. She reminded him that Jesus was a carpenter, and she told him that one of the greatest stories of all time was set in a garden. The Garden of Eden. When he didn't laugh, she told him step one in him learning how to get along with others would be him learning how to get over himself.

There'd been one guy at St. Jude's whom Kyle got on OK with. A single guy. Patrick Bogardus. They'd run into him alone at a restaurant one Friday night, and Sara had invited the guy to have dinner with them. After that Kyle golfed with Patrick a few times, headed to Wrigley with him one afternoon to drink a few beers in the sun, and now and then Patrick invited Kyle to his apartment to watch a game. Of all the men he could've buddied up with at St. Jude's, Kyle had to pick one without a wife. He knows that's what Sara thought. Whenever he left for Patrick's, Sara would make a comment about "the bachelor pad." Kyle imagined Sara imagining lava lamps, black lights, leather beanbag chairs, a pinball machine and a full bar.

But Patrick's apartment wasn't like that at all. He had a place near Old Town, and it was classy and clean. Patrick was into art, and he was a neat housekeeper. He brewed his own beer to boot, and it was pretty good. The last time Kyle was over, only a few weeks before Patrick was to leave town—he was being transferred—there was a fresh batch of lager to try. Patrick served the beer in juice glasses, sipped it like wine, and with pen and paper in hand, solicited Kyle's feedback.

After the beer that night, Patrick got up from the couch where he and Kyle were sitting and took down a vase from the fireplace mantel. He reached in and produced a bag of marijuana and some rolling papers. "You smoke?" he said to Kyle as he rolled a joint on the coffee table.

"Wow. No," Kyle said. "Not since college." He leaned back and stretched his arms and neck to show that he was relaxed, unfazed. "Not even then really."

"You're driving, and we've already had beer, so I won't suggest you partake, but if you wanted to make the suggestion yourself...." Patrick took a lighter out of a drawer on the coffee table and brought the joint to his lips. After he hit it, he leaned over and offered it to Kyle, who smiled and shook his head. Patrick shrugged his shoulders, exhaled and then took another hit. "You're a good man," he said.

Kyle stayed another couple hours to listen to Patrick, who suddenly had a lot to say, much of it surprising and personal. Afterward Kyle wondered if Patrick had planned to unburden himself that night or if it had just happened. He also wondered if Patrick felt OK the next morning about having shared so much. Kyle couldn't help but suspect that Patrick had some regrets, especially because Patrick never called again, not even to say goodbye.

Patrick told Kyle three things that night. First, he told him the truth about why he was leaving Chicago. He hadn't really been transferred; rather, he'd quit. If he stayed, starting next month, he'd be subject to random drug testing. "Bullshit I can't abide," he'd said. "A matter of principle." Second, he admitted to Kyle that he often attended Sunday services at St. Jude's stoned. He talked about how much better the worship experience was for him while under the influence. The music, the homily, even the Eucharist. By better he meant fuller, deeper. "I'm able to get out of my head so God can get in," he said. Finally, Patrick told Kyle that he was in love with someone he couldn't have, someone who lived far away, that this had been the case for nearly a decade, and he thought he was reaching the end of his rope.

"This woman," Kyle had asked. "Why can't you have her?"

"Woman," Patrick said, and he pressed the heel of his hand into his eye like he was trying to hold back tears. "It's more complicated than the most complicated thing you've ever heard of," he said, and he shook his head. "Bless you for asking, though."

The obvious question didn't arise then, but Kyle finds himself posing it now as he drifts off into a nap over the head of his wife and her dinner guests and their Cornish hens, and when he wakes up forty-five minutes later, the question's still in his head. What's the most complicated thing he's ever heard of? He has no idea what the answer might be to this question.

Kyle sits up in bed and listens. Nothing. Everyone's gone. Sara's pulled it off.

He thinks about switching on the TV, but the remote isn't on his bed stand, and it's not on Sara's either. Kyle's suspicion is that Sara hid it so he wouldn't be tempted.

Kyle rises to his feet with the notion of heading to the kitchen to make himself some toast. He's still a little dizzy but definitely on the mend. Even though he's famished, and he imagines there are leftovers in the fridge, he knows he needs to go slowly, start small.

He's in the kitchen removing the twist tie from the bread bag when he hears the toilet flush. He freezes, unsure what to do, and in a few seconds Brangwynne Koonce is standing in the doorway looking at him. She's brandishing a star on her chest, like she's the sheriff of something.

"Kyle," Brangwynne says, taking in his boxers, undershirt and black socks. "We missed you tonight."

"How were the hens?" Kyle says. "Sara was hoping they wouldn't be too dry." He puts the toaster cozy back onto the toaster. He works the twist tie back onto the bread bag and studies the nutrition information. Seventy calories a slice. First ingredient is water.

"Perfectly not dry," Brangwynne says. She scratches her hip lazily and a smile grows on her face. "My hen was a perfect hen. And the wine, too. The wine was perfect wine. And your wife. Your wife is a perfect wife, and she's waiting for me outside in her car. She tells me that she's my ride for the rest of the night." Brangwynne giggles a little and starts to turn around, then stops. "Could I ask you something, Kyle? I hope this doesn't sound too whatever."

"Sure. OK," Kyle says. "Shoot."

"Patrick Bogardus." Brangwynne pauses to clear her throat and trace with her thumb the star on her chest. "He ever mention me?"

dessert

Ann was already up drinking coffee when the sun rose this morning. The post-storm scene outside the dining room window was breathtaking. There wasn't a hint of wind, and in the park across the street, the ice-glazed trees glared so brightly they were hard to look at. Garrett didn't come downstairs until just before noon, and until then, Ann sat at the dining room table studying the icescape, lazing over the newspaper, and making her grocery list. In addition to the regular weekly shopping, she'd have to get stuff for the pies she was making. The progressive dinner's tonight.

The morning before, Ann doubted there would be a progressive dinner. She'd tried to do the shopping then, but made it only halfway to the store before chickening out and returning home. She'd thought she'd be able to beat the snow and ice if she hustled—the people on The Weather Channel are always overly nervous, always crying wolf—but the wind was already whipping something fierce, and on the horizon she could see the storm advancing off the lake. The Lakefront Trail had already been closed off with tape and barriers, but in one spot near the zoo, she'd seen kids ducking under, some with bikes and some without, the water lapping up onto the concrete just short of their feet. Some of the bike-riding kids weren't wearing helmets. A couple weren't even wearing hats. Ann wondered aloud where the kids' parents were, why the kids weren't in school.

This morning, out her kitchen window, it was a more familiar group of kids. The neighborhood contingent, the usual suspects, out in the park full-force. Ann was impressed by how they got busy right away, gathering fallen branches to make a fort. The parents of these kids had to threaten them regularly with various indignities and penalties to motivate them to do the simplest of tasks—Ann's heard the exchanges, and depending on the tone of voice has either grinned or winced—but early this morning, hauling wet wood around a park, these kids looked like they couldn't get enough of work.

For most of the kids, though, the novelty wore off rather quickly. Of course it did. They began to take long breaks from fort-building for slush wars and games of tag. For a few of the kids, though, building the fort was serious business, and they came up with a good design. They built two lean-to's facing each other and used brush to span the gap between the two structures. Ann was reminded of those longhouses the Iroquois built.

When the worker kids finished the fort, the more play-minded kids wanted to play in it right along with them. Of course this happened. And, of course, the worker kids balked. There was yelling, name-calling, threats of tattling, and then there was an advance on the fort. The worker kids were badly outnumbered, so it was over in a matter of minutes. One kid stood up under the low roof, bringing the fort down around him, and then a wrestling match broke out in one of the lean-to's, and that came down. The second lean-to eventually collapsed, too. It was one of the worker kids who knocked it down, though, and she did so purposefully. Fell on her sword. Out of resignation and frustration. Ann admired her a little.

Ann wonders if that's it for the fort-building, or if there will be a second act somewhere down the line. She'd like to think the fort builders will get a second wind and take another crack at it. Eventually city maintenance workers will descend on the park with their bush-hogs, chainsaws and wood chippers, but that won't be until spring, which, in winter, always seems an eternity away.

After grocery shopping, Ann spends the afternoon baking pies. It's just getting dark outside when she pulls them out of the oven and Garrett enters the kitchen to dispense information. In England, it turns out, a progressive dinner is called a safari supper. The British version incorporates many more guests and hosts, is much more complicated. It requires more extensive planning, tighter scheduling. Dining stations serve simultaneously, and at each course, you eat with a different group of people. At each stop you get an envelope giving you your next assignment. Everyone is decidedly not in the same boat. Sometimes couples are even split up. The luck of the draw is part of the fun.

"Someone's been on Wikipedia," Ann says.

"Plus, I'm ready for Peter and his wack-a-doo idea about re-reversing the flow of the river to keep Asian carp out of the lake," Garrett says. "I've got facts and figures. Did you know that in winter the river already flows in both directions? At the surface, it flows away from the lake, but down deep, near the riverbed, the water travels toward the lake."

"I did know that," Ann says. "I'm sure Peter does, too. Even if he doesn't, he'll tell you he does, and then he'll come up with something that he hopes you don't know."

"The pies look incredible," Garrett says. He puts his hands on Ann's shoulders and kisses the top of her head.

"Apple, cherry, lemon meringue, shoo-fly," Ann says.

"I approve," Garrett says. "I should probably go throw more salt on the sidewalk. I bet we got an inch-and-a-half of ice last night, and it's starting to refreeze now. Getting treacherous again."

"What's a broken neck or two among friends?" Ann says.

"That's right," Garrett says. "OK."

Ann knows her comment didn't register. Things like company pre-occupy Garrett. He drifts in and out of listening mode. He's the first to admit it. Ann sometimes resents his quick and easy admissions, wonders if they get him off the hook too easily, wonders if a little denial now and then, a little back-and-forth once in a while, might not be healthy.

Once the guests arrive, sit down, and have their pie orders filled—Ann predicts apple will be most popular, shoo-fly least—Ann knows that her husband, Reverend Garrett Tudor, shepherd of the flock at St. Jude's Episcopal Church, will hold forth with the safari supper material. His inclination in conversation is to lead, and he prepares himself accordingly. Even when it's just the two of them sitting down to leftovers in the middle of the week, he always seems to have one or two subjects already in mind, a clear idea of how he wants conversation to play out.

Ann doesn't bake often. This is in part because Garrett's watching his triglycerides and in part because baking reminds her too much of her first husband. Her late husband. Many things in Ann's life remind her of Nathaniel, but baking brings him back too fully. Especially when they were newlyweds, Ann and Nat often baked together on weekends. Money was tight when they were young, and baking together, and then eating what they baked, was a relatively cheap date. Nat, who'd grown up in a house where men stayed out of the kitchen, couldn't get enough. He appreciated the process as much as if not more than the product, and when they treated other couples to their creations, Nat was stubborn about sharing recipes. "Magicians don't give away their secrets," he'd say. When Ann would assert that baking was more chemistry than magic, he'd reply that he was fairly certain chemists didn't give away their secrets either.

So now, a decade-and-a-half after his death, Ann finds herself on the verge of talking out loud to him as she cracks eggs, wields measuring spoons, and rolls out dough. This impulse unnerves her. Talking to ghosts is something people do on their deathbeds. As Nat had neared the end, he'd more than once cooed for Merle, his beloved beagle, who'd been gone five years. It had hurt Nat and Ann so much when Merle died that they'd sworn off dogs.

This is Ann and Garrett's tenth anniversary year, and she'd gotten to ten years with Nat before he passed, so as it stands now, it's a tie. She's as much Garrett's wife as Nat's. Garrett is as much her husband as Nat was.

This kind of thinking, Ann doesn't imagine it can lead anywhere good. She knows it's not something she'd share with anyone, and she figures that's a good indication she shouldn't be thinking about it. Recently, though, it's been hard not to. Today the baking, but before that, last Sunday, is when the seed was planted. The Year B lectionary reading for the third Sunday after Epiphany.

In Ann's opinion, Garrett took the easy way out in his sermon by ignoring Paul's First Letter to the Corinthians and focusing instead on the Old Testament and Gospel readings. Jonah, fresh from the whale and grumpy, finally delivers his message of fire and brimstone to the Ninevites, who, in turn, repent, and God shows mercy. And then in the Gospel of Mark, Jesus heads down to the Galilean docks and starts recruiting disciples, his "fishers of men." Grace and salvation. Feel-good stuff. Affirming and familiar. Spiritual comfort food.

St. Paul's words from I Corinthians, though, are of a different variety. Mourners should cut out their mourning, happy people should sober up, and married people should forget their spouses. Why? Because this world is on its way out. No metaphor here to hide behind. No wiggle room. Ann would've liked to hear Garrett's spin.

Of all the available notions of heaven, the one Ann comes closest to believing in is the personal heaven, the tailor-fitted paradise. When Nat passed, more than a few of Ann's church friends suggested she read C.S. Lewis' *A Grief Observed*. Empathy was why. Lewis had lost his wife to cancer and in the book posed to God the sort of anger-tinged existential questions that Ann's friends assumed must've been haunting her. What most intrigued Ann about Lewis, though—she'd gone on to read a few more of his books—wasn't his widower status and pain as much as it was his ruminations on the afterlife. Lewis likes to think marriage bonds might stay intact somehow, goes as far as to propose that entire families and households, beloved pets included, might be reconstituted, like orange juice. When Ann remembers this idea now, she thinks of old Merle, imagines him curled at her feet as she sits on the middle cushion of a celestial couch, smack-dab between Nat and Garrett.

Ann isn't the kind of person to laugh out loud much, neither alone nor with other people—she's more of a grinner, more apt to say "That's funny" than she is to actually giggle—but this version of her afterlife has her laughing so hard and so suddenly that she has to put both hands on the kitchen counter for support. When Garrett re-enters, he's stunned into laughing along with her. Ann shifts from the kitchen counter to Garrett, wraps her arms around him and is laughing tears onto his cold neck when the doorbell rings.

An hour later, the group that inhabits Ann's house is a bit more rag-tag than she'd expected. They didn't all come together—the doorbell rang three different times—and some of them seem a little sleepy even though it's not yet nine o'clock. The final couple to arrive, Brangwynne Koonce and Sara Lutz, came armed with half-empty bottles of wine left over from the previous courses. If there's another progressive dinner in the future, Ann thinks designated drivers might not be a bad idea. Or maybe a walking tour.

An hour-and-a-half after the guests arrive, they're gone. The pies were a hit, even the shoo-fly, and after serving two pots of coffee, Ann felt better about dismissing everyone. She abstained herself because coffee doesn't agree with her at night. Not so much because of the caffeine—she'd brewed decaf, too—but because it gives her heartburn. She has that in common with Garrett. Nat, though, would drink the stuff from sunup to sundown. Man had a stomach like cast iron.

As Ann finishes the dishes—Garrett had offered to help, but she'd sent him up to bed, to channel-surf himself asleep—she wonders if heaven might require her to make a decision between Nat and Garrett. Ladies' choice, like a Sadie Hawkins dance. And then she wonders if there might be a third option offered, if she might not rather do heaven single. Unmanned. While quiet and sometimes lonely, those five years that Ann had on her own between Nat's passing and getting together with Garrett weren't alto-gether unsatisfactory. She wouldn't necessarily trade them in.

In Ann's opinion, the most entertaining guests this evening had been Brangwynne Koonce and Sara Lutz. Ann watched them all night. The only women without men attached, they'd stuck to each other. At one point they interlocked their arms and fed each other pie; at another point Ann saw Sara brush back Brangwynne's hair before whispering into her ear, and whatever she whispered made Brangwynne fall over forward and giggle on Sara's shoulder. Ann hadn't even known the two women were friends, and suddenly they were acting like tipsy sorority sisters. On some level it made sense. Ann had suspected both of having crushes on Patrick Bogardus before he left town, so they had that in common. They weren't the only ones, either. On Sunday afternoons after church, Ann and Garrett would chuckle about it. Garrett had said that Patrick, if he wanted, could start a very successful niche ministry for middle-aged women, both single and married alike. It felt OK to joke about because it was all so obviously harmless. It takes two to tango, and Patrick, while polite and personable, clearly had no interest in any of the women. He appeared dedicated to flying solo.

As Ann closes up the house and turns off the lights before heading upstairs, she realizes how tired she is. She'd spent the night before on the couch. Garrett had been in and out of bed with stomach trouble, and on top of that, of course, there had been the storm. Crashing branches. Sleet pinging the windows. Thunder in January. Not stuff made for sleeping through. Ann's not sure she slept at all. Has no idea how she'll sleep tonight.

OLD ROUTE 61

In the beginning, the carrier would cradle the corpse to his chest as he made his way down the smoldering road. He'd walk as far as he could, a few steps, before his arms and back began to bark, and then he'd lay the corpse down in a cluster of crabgrass or pigweed or foxtail off the heat-buckled shoulder of the abandoned highway, and there the corpse would wait while he rested.

The carrier wouldn't sit to rest. Tired and drunk as he was, he knew sitting was a slippery slope: it could lead to lying down, and lying down to sleep, and sleep wasn't something he could afford, so instead of sitting he'd crouch, balance on the balls of his feet and lean over his lap, his elbows resting on his thighs, until his legs ached. When he'd stand himself back up, he wouldn't feel all the way drunk anymore, but he'd feel like he had to retch, and he'd suppose getting the retching over with might bring him a measure of relief, so he'd walk a few feet further up the roadside to bow over a patch of crownvetch or loosestrife or wild rose, and stick his finger down his throat, and his stomach would lurch, and his ribs would heave, and he'd belch and strain, but nothing would come up, and rather than feeling better for his efforts, he'd feel worse. He'd then take the flask out of his jacket pocket and look at it like he didn't know from where it had come or to whom it belonged, its presence a mystery, and he'd warn himself about how much further he had to go and remind himself of how poorly he felt, but then he'd surprise himself by taking a short pull anyway, and then, tortured with regret and dread, he'd roughly wipe his mouth on the cuff of his jacket before surprising himself again by taking a longer pull.

So the carrier would make his way thusly, in fits and starts, experimenting with different ways of carrying the corpse, of negotiating the awkward weight of it. He'd try carrying the corpse to one side, pressed against his hip and ribs like a satchel, and then he'd swing it around and press it to his other side, but walking lopsided like this allowed for only baby steps over the fractured spine of the feverish road, and the slower his progress, the more troubled the carrier would become about the coal and gas-fed fire beneath his feet, the decades-old heat working its way up through the earth to reclaim him. He'd now and then think he smelled the soles of his boots melting, and here and there he'd catch half-glimpses of flames flickering in the cauldron-like potholes he stepped over and around, and then he would shift the corpse to piggyback or drape it over one shoulder and try to pick up the pace, but nothing the carrier tried would allow him to move as quickly as he needed to move, as quickly as one needs to move with an old yet unbroken fire underfoot.

Each time the carrier would stop to rest and surprise himself with the flask, he'd lay the corpse on the roadside, and each time the carrier would rise out of his crouch to recommence carrying, the corpse would feel heavier, as if it had somehow gained bulk just by lying in damp weeds, and the carrier would decide that not only was the carrying whipping him, but the resting was whipping him, too, so he'd swear off rest, and before long the carrier would become too tired to take even one more step, and he'd collapse.

At this point, of course, it would come to pass that the carrier and the corpse would become each the other, the well-rested corpse resurrecting to relieve the exhausted carrier, and the exhausted carrier succumbing once more to the hard-earned repose and comfort of death. And so it would continue to come to pass, over and over thusly, the carrier and the corpse becoming each the other, and then each the other again, and then again, until the scorched highway would finally come to an abrupt end at the bulldozed embankment, over which the carrier, hauling the corpse, would climb.

On the other side, when the carrier's boots would meet the cool, smooth blacktop of the new highway, the corpse would awaken, ease himself out of the carrier's arms, gather himself upright on his own feet, and the two figures, now each bearing the burden of only himself, side by side on the new highway's roomy shoulder, would pass the never empty flask back and forth, and turn to face the headlights of the oncoming traffic, and stick out their thumbs.

PART I

The Prophet, 1969

He baits the first trap of the season with parsnips, the second with the musk of the first trap's yield. How things wind on, how they progress.

The muskrat is unclean, and the raccoon is unclean, and the mink is unclean, and the fox is unclean, but through him all becomes clean. The prophet eats them clean, transubstantiates them clean. He strips them clean, sells their clean skins. But all these things, flesh and skin and money, will pass away, and after all things have passed away, it shall come to pass that nothing shall pass away.

The day of fulfillment draws near.

The prophet is not. He is not the author of the truth. Rather, he is its knower, its agent, its arbiter. He measures it and discerns it, not for the sake of himself or for others, but for the sake of the truth itself. The truth is part and parcel. It feeds on the prophet like fuel. It blazes up and engulfs him. It burns cleanest when the prophet comes to it clear-minded and undistracted, when he's able to empty himself and be nothing but fuel. Sometimes whiskey helps. It brings him to sleep, and in sleep he's at his emptiest. In sleep he is skinned clean. In sleep he can best awaken and be awakened by the truth, and in sleep he can best fill it and be filled by it. This, the empty fullness of sleep, the full emptiness of sleep, the skinless cleanness of sleep, is part of the truth.

The day of fulfillment draws near.

Of course the truth had always been. It lived in the book and in the earth and in the streams that watered the earth and in the gathered waters and in every creature that crawled and crept across the earth and in every creature that swam and flew, but the life of the truth was a slept one. Like a seed, the truth hibernated, dreamt a long dormant dream of itself until the prophet roused it into sprouting, transformed it from sleeping truth into awakened truth by knowing it and claiming it and keeping it. Like a secret.

Whatever it takes, the prophet will do. Whatever it takes to preserve the coming of the day of fulfillment.

The truth comes like a thief in the night. Like a muskrat in the night. Black-eyed and slick-coated. The truth is in the clover-covered bank, and the truth is in the cattail nest, and the truth is in the trap. The truth is in the self-sharpening teeth, and the truth is in the bubbles under the ice, and the truth is in the 'V' of the snout-parted water.

There is today's partial truth, fragile and transitory, and there is tomorrow's whole truth, final and determinant. There is dust, and there are ashes. There is the fire and what can now be known of it, its smoke and heat, and there is what is yet to be known, its light and flames. There is the skin, and there is what's under the skin. There is the lion's den, the leper's cave, the valley of the dry bones. There is the desert, the wilderness, the belly of the whale. There is the fiery furnace. There is the mud-hole. There is the mine. There is the tomb. There is the cleft of the rock. There is the crevice. There is the flood and the rainbow. There is the promised land and the broken promise. There is honor for the prophet, save for in his own country.

The day of fulfillment draws near.

Philip, 1976

After pulling into his driveway, Philip turns off the truck but stays in his seat. He lights a cigarette, the last one in the pack, and then takes his jackknife out of his pocket and carefully works the blade over the flecks of blue and white paint that spatter his fingernails.

He's in no hurry to get inside. Joanne's inside, and he has to tell her his plans for the weekend, and she's not going to like them—Philip understands why; he doesn't like them either—but he has no choice. After the mortgage payment is made early next week, they'll be about busted, and the job he's working now won't pay for another three weeks. Joanne will have to go grocery shopping at least once before that. "I'm going in the hole to get us out of the hole." That's what Philip will say to broach the subject. He'll try to keep it lighthearted, upbeat. See how that goes.

When Philip and Joanne first married, they both used to smoke in the house, but when Todd came along and Joanne quit, Philip's smoking got moved outside. Now that's Todd's practically grown—Philip knows the boy has his own cigarettes, even knows where he hides them—Philip could move his smoking back inside if he wanted, but he figures he'll keep things as is. He's gotten used to a clean-smelling house, and he knows what cigarettes can do to a paint job. Plus he likes how he smokes outside. He doesn't watch TV and smoke, or read and smoke, or listen to records and smoke. He just smokes. Each cigarette seems to count more this way, so he ends up smoking less. He knows he needs to smoke less. What with him not getting any younger. What with the monthly household budget gone to hell.

Todd's going to want to work Sensenig's mine with Philip this weekend, and Philip's going to need him. This will be Joanne's least favorite part of Philip's weekend plans. Todd's gone to Sensenig's with Philip before, but only to watch. This time, though, he'll have to pitch in. Sensenig's son-in-law broke his collar bone a few weeks ago, a casualty of a Labor Day picnic wheelbarrow race, so they'll need a third set of hands. Philip had suggested a few other candidates to Sensenig—he had a few guys who owed him favors—but Sensenig wasn't keen on the idea of letting anyone new in on his operation. The mine had been in his family for close to fifty years, and he was guarded about it. Call it a bootleg mine around him, he'll wave a correcting finger in your face, tell you what he has is a private mine, tell you to go pound salt with your bootleg. Philip's been helping out Sensenig at the mine once or twice a year since he was Todd's age. He won't get rich this weekend, but Sensenig's pay is more than fair. At any rate, this will be the last time. Philip will make sure Joanne knows this. Final go round. Never again. Mrs. Sensenig's finally convinced her husband to buy an oil furnace.

A couple of working weekends at the mine with a three- or four-man crew usually gets Sensenig five tons of coal, more than what he needs to get himself through the winter, so he gives the rest away. Mostly to old-timers, older than himself even. Between what he gives away and what he pays his workers, Phillip figures Sensenig hasn't saved all that much money over the years burning coal instead of oil or gas, but he understands it's not about the money for the old man. It's about keeping up work he likes doing, work he did with his father and grandfather, and it's some about being a good neighbor. Philip suspects Sensenig's asking him to work the mine this weekend is just as much about neighborliness as anything else. Philip had told Sensenig about the roof last week when they'd seen each other at the diner, and then just today Sensenig had tracked Philip down at his job site to ask him if he could help out this weekend. Made it like Philip would be the one doing him the favor. Philip's appreciative.

When Philip climbs out of his truck, he doesn't head inside to Joanne right away. Instead, he walks down the driveway, crosses the road, wanders a few yards into the spongy earth of the fallow field, and then turns back around to look at his house. His new half-a-roof. He holds his cigarette in his lips and hoods his eyes with his hands. Zuccari told him it wouldn't be too obvious—he'd done his best to match the old shingle color—but it's obvious to Philip. A house divided.

He and Joanne hadn't had enough saved to get the whole thing done. When Philip called Zuccari, his hope was that re-pitching around the chimney would solve the problem—they'd been getting some water in the attic after thaws and heavy rains over the past year—but when Zuccari climbed his ladder to see what was what, he found water pooling in more than a few places, and here and there the wood under the shingles was rotten. More than just a patch job. Zuccari told Philip and Joanne they could roll the dice, pray for a light winter, try to make do until spring, but he couldn't recommend putting it off. He seemed genuinely sorry about having to deliver this news even though it meant money in his pocket. When Joanne offered him a cup of coffee, he refused. Didn't even want a glass of water. "Don't want to trouble you," he said.

"Then tell us our roof looks like new," Philip said. "Tell us everything's shipshape. That would be no trouble at all."

"What do you think of this?" Zuccari said without smiling. "I could re-pitch and re-flash the chimney and the west side of the house now, and then I could do the rest come spring. The eastern half of your roof could maybe wait that long. It's not quite as bad because it's in the shade of your two big maples. People think rain, wind and snow are what do in a roof, but it's the sun, really. Roofs burn up."

So that's what Joanne and Philip decided. Still, the bill for the half-roof about wiped them out, and a good chunk of the money they'd been waiting on from Joanne's mother—she'd passed a couple months before—was now already good as spent with Zuccari scheduled to come around again in the spring.

Philip flicks the butt of his cigarette into the field and re-crosses the road back to the house. You think you might get ahead a little now and then, but it never lasts. When Zuccari had given his estimate for the job, Philip tried to lower the number by suggesting he'd be willing to do some painting for Zuccari down the road, but Zuccari told him renovation jobs were slow in coming these days, and, besides, he needed cash to pay his crew. Things were tight for him, too. Seemed to Philip that everyone he knew was scraping. He'd like the opportunity to be spiteful of someone, to begrudge them their wealth and comfort, but he couldn't think of even one person. Not around here, anyway.

Philip knows one reason why Zuccari's getting fewer jobs. It's the same for him with painting. It's not just President Ford or Governor Shapp, either. Not just inflation. Not just gas prices. People around here feel like they're in limbo. How smart is it to spend money on a paint job or a thirty-year roof when there's a fire raging beneath your house? Even those like Philip who believe the whole thing is probably overblown can't help but think twice. He talked to a guy at the diner the other day who told him the fire was headed for an underground creek, and that when it hit there, that would be all she wrote, people would have to make up some new problem to worry about, and Philip felt all right about things for a while after that, but when he mentioned this to Joanne, she told him she'd heard about the underground creek from a teller at the bank, but the teller went on to say that it would be nothing for a big, hot coal seam fire to jump a creek. What's more, Joanne told Philip she'd heard there wasn't just one fire anymore. The original blaze had branched off, multiplied. However many old mining tunnels there were under the town, that's how many fires. Things were burning in every direction now.

Philip climbs the porch steps and sees Joanne in profile through the small window on top of the door, scrubbing potatoes at the sink. Her mouth is moving. She could be singing or talking to herself. Could be praying. Something she does. Whatever she's doing is making her smile.

Philip turns around, descends the steps and walks to the shed in the backyard. He ducks through the door and heads for the shelf on the rear wall that holds his and Todd's tackle boxes. He opens Todd's, finds the almost new pack of Pall Malls among the spinners and spoons, and shakes loose two cigarettes. He lights one, sticks the other behind his ear, makes space for himself between his and Todd's fishing rods and leans back against the wall.

He's not halfway through the cigarette when the door creaks open and Todd walks in. The boy takes a step or two before he raises his eyes and sees Philip, and when he does he jumps, gives a startled grunt. His hands fly up over his shoulders, like he's surrendering.

"What are you so jittery for?" Philips says through a smile. "Feeling guilty about something?"

"Damn!" Todd says and cups both hands over his heart. "What are you doing in here?"

"Same thing you're doing," Philip says. He takes the cigarette out from behind his ear and holds it out to his son.

Todd takes the cigarette, jerks his head back and to the side to get the hair out of his eyes, and produces a lighter from the pocket of his jean jacket. "I wish I didn't have to hide them," Todd says.

"Oh, these are yours?" Philip says.

"Seems silly to me," Todd says. "Having to sneak around. You smoke. You started younger than me."

"Tell your mother that," Philip says. "And then do me a favor and tell her I need you to help me this weekend."

"Yeah?" Todd says. "Doing what?"

"Working over to Sensenig's."

Todd jerks his head again, runs his fingers back through his hair and tucks it behind his ears. "Yeah? Cool."

"Tell your mother that," Philip says. "Tell her it's cool."

"The coal hole," Todd says, trying to imitate Sensenig's snarly voice. He bends at the waist, hunches his shoulders. "It's cool, Mom. I'll be helping out Dad at the coal hole. The goddam coal hole."

"You done?" Philip says. He fights a smirk. "Respect your elders. You ever hear that one? Does that ring a bell?"

"I'm not disrespecting Sensenig. I'm imitating him," Todd says. The boy lifts his chin and blows a perfect ring into the air, and he and Philip watch it float up into the cobwebs that decorate the shed's ceiling. "Imitation is like flattery."

"You need a haircut," Philip says. "Sensenig won't even let you on his property with your luxurious locks hanging in your face. And by the way, just for the record, I've known for at least three months about your cigarettes."

"I'll pull it back with a rubber band. No big deal," Todd says. "And just for the record, I knew you knew."

Sy, 1984

"Sy," she'd say into my ear, and she'd say it like a sigh. I'd be sitting at the desk in my office, and she'd sneak up behind me. When I'd jump, she'd put her hands on my shoulders and laugh. At me. At her play on words. This was the beginning.

When I hired her, it was the furthest thing from my mind. I'd want Beth to know this, to know I hadn't schemed or planned. I hired Vonda because I needed help. It probably wouldn't be for long—I knew the town was on its last legs—but with the upheaval and uncertainty in the air, people were suddenly looking to take care of business, tie up loose ends, before they started the next chapters of their lives. I was up to my neck in work. Drafting wills, finalizing divorces, negotiating property line disputes. Vonda was waiting for me at the office door, résumé and letters of reference in hand, on the morning of the first and only day the ad appeared in the paper. She'd put in a year of law school at Dickinson, had worked a while for a CPA, and had plenty of typing and filing experience.

"What happened after Dickinson?" I said. We were still standing up. I hadn't even taken off my jacket yet.

"I got married, and then I got pregnant, and then I lost the baby," she said. "I wasn't able to bounce back as quickly as I wanted to, as quickly as my professors wanted me to."

I hired her on the spot. It was a no-brainer.

What happened between her and me didn't happen all of a sudden. It smoldered a while. I knew I was in trouble when I started to wait for it, to anticipate and look forward to Vonda's breath in my ear—"Sy"—her breath on my neck, and then I wouldn't jump. I'd lean back into my name. "At your service," I'd say—something dumb like that, something that didn't sound right coming from me, that made me sound like I was reciting lines someone else had written—and she'd still laugh, but differently, and she'd linger there for a moment behind me after she was done laughing, but as soon as I'd start to turn that would be her cue to walk away.

We were all business face to face. It was behind my back that we started to lose track of ourselves.

The first time was a Saturday morning. I'd come in for a couple hours each weekend to clean the office. Vacuum, dust, take care of the bathroom. I didn't want to pay a service, partly because of the cost, but partly because I'd gone that route before, and I hadn't been happy. The office didn't get as clean as when I cleaned it myself. Makes sense. Something is yours, you take care of it. You take care of it better than if it weren't yours.

Vonda had left her umbrella Friday afternoon. That's why she showed up that Saturday morning, she said. She needed her umbrella even though the rain was yesterday's news, the sky was clear, and the weather forecast called for more of the same as far into the future as could be seen. Later she told me she left the umbrella on purpose and played a game with herself. She told herself she'd swing by Saturday morning at ten-thirty to pick it up, and if I weren't there that would be a sign, and if I were, that would be a sign, too.

"Since you're here, could you take a letter?" I said. "Just real quick?"

She looked at me like I was teasing, but when she saw I was serious, she put her umbrella back in the corner and sat down behind the new word processor I'd just bought her. Auto-correct and word-wrap. Letter-quality printing. Memory store for up to three pages of copy. She turned it on, set up a piece of letterhead. The machine hummed quietly under her fingers.

"Dear Vonda," I began, and her shoulders shook a little. My hands were on the back of her chair, and she reached back to cover them with her hands. "Dear Vonda," I said again. "Where will we be a year from now?" I meant it. I wanted an answer. More than half the town had already fled the fire at this point, had already abandoned their homes and taken the relocation money from the government to make their lives elsewhere. Ashland and Mt. Carmel and Shamokin and Sunbury and Harrisburg and Philadelphia and Baltimore and New York and D.C. Even most of those who remained were making plans to leave. There were only a few of us who had no intentions of moving. Some of us because we smelled a conspiracy in the works and wanted to stand up against the powers-that-be. Some of us, though, had less principled reasons for staying. Maybe we wanted to see if the relocation allowances would get any bigger. Or maybe we couldn't think of anywhere better to go. Or maybe for some of us an underground fire was the least of our problems.

When Vonda stood and turned, I saw she was crying, and I thought I'd made a mistake, and I thought this when she passed me on her way to the freshly cleaned bathroom, and I thought this a few minutes later when she came out, not crying now. I thought this after she put her lips on mine, and after we moved each other to my office, to my desk, and after we took turns stopping each other and then starting up again. I felt like this when we were done, as we dressed, as she left. I felt like this a half-hour after she was gone when I noticed she'd forgotten her umbrella again. I felt other things, too—and these things were stronger and eventually outmuscled everything else—but I never stopped suspecting myself of having made a mistake. Not even the thrill I felt could completely bury that. Not even the joy.

Gabe, 1995

"If not twins, you at least must be sisters," Gabe says. He wears a short-sleeved polo with the name of his employer, Weis Markets, stamped over his heart. "You both have the same look on your faces. Kind of half-bitchy. But cute, though. You must at least be cousins."

"You're a tool, Gabe," the taller girl says. She doesn't turn her whole body to answer the boy—she can't be bothered—but she swings her head back a little, just enough to give him a glimpse of her profile. "You've been going to school with us since kindergarten, so you know we aren't related. What you might not know about Jillie and me, though, is that we're lovers. Want to watch?"

"You're just encouraging him," Jillie says to her friend, "and he doesn't need encouragement."

"That's right. School. I thought I knew you girls from somewhere," Gabe says. He lifts another case of cereal boxes off his cart and slices it open with his utility knife. "OK, sure. You're Jillie and Tammy, the girls who were always staring at me in homeroom last year. Like you were in heat or something."

"In your dreams, Gabe," Tammy says, fighting a grin. "Jillie and me were hot for you in your dreams."

"And then you woke up with sticky sheets," Jillie adds, and the two girls laugh and slap hands.

"I think you were the least impressive boy in our homeroom," Tammy says as she takes Jillie's arm in hers. "Maybe in our whole graduating class. Your legs are kind of stumpy, and you're kind of weird looking in the face, and you're not very bright."

"If that's true," Gabe says, "how come the summer before 9th grade at Kyle LaRoche's birthday party you let me—"

"Ninth grade?" Tammy interrupts. "Really? Live in the past much?"

"I don't know why Jeannette puts up with you," Jillie says. "Nice girlfriend like that, way out of your league, and here you are trying to flirt with us."

"You guys are the flirters. I'm the flirtee," Gabe says, turning back to his cart. "I'm just a working man, filling shelves with Corn Flakes and Sugar Smacks, trying to save money for college, trying to build a better future for myself through putting in an honest day's labor, and you temptresses come by trying to distract me."

"You're such a victim," Tammy says.

"I'm bored with this," Jillie says. "I'm bored with this yesterday."

"We have other aisles in this store," Gabe says. "Eleven of them, in fact. This is the only one I'm in at present."

Before the girls are out of sight, Jillie can't resist one more look back at Gabe. One more grin. She'd be fun, Gabe thinks. If he didn't have Jeannette. A different Gabe, a Gabe without a girlfriend like Jeannette, could have fun with Jillie.

Gabe looks at his watch. Time crawls in this place. Even when he's goofing off. It's like time works differently inside the store than it does anywhere else in the world, and every time he looks at his watch he's newly discouraged by this fact. Every morning getting ready for work he tells himself not to wear his watch, but he puts it on anyway—part of him is scared that without it, time wouldn't move at all—and every time he looks at it during his shift he tells himself that's the last time, but it's never the last time. Jugger makes fun of him for it, says if it were up to him Gabe's pay would get docked a quarter every time he looked at his watch, but Jugger takes smoke breaks every hour, and he's always checking the scanner he keeps in the back room and the pager he keeps on his belt, hoping for a fire or some other emergency he can take off for. Gabe figures if he were going to stay on at Weis's, make a career out of it like Jugger, he'd probably take up smoking and sign up to run into burning buildings for no pay, too.

Twenty-one more days until he heads off to Kutztown. Of those, he's scheduled to spend seventeen here at the store. Could be more if someone gets sick or calls off for whatever reason. On days he's not scheduled at Weis's, he tries to get two workouts in—morning and afternoon—unless Jeannette's off from her job at the vet and they can spend the day together. It seems their days off almost never match up this summer, though. What's more, on top of work and workouts and trying to see Jeannette, he's soon going to need to find some time to start packing. When Gabe leaves, Scott, his younger brother, is going to move into his room, and his mom's planning on making Scott's old room her new sewing space, so everything Gabe isn't taking with him to college or throwing away he has to lug up to the attic. At any rate, even his days off aren't shaping up to be days off.

Twenty-one days. Gabe figures if he stays the course, if he keeps cramming himself full of bananas and protein shakes in between meals and keeps up with the weights, he might be able to add another four or five pounds. That would get him up close to one-sixty-five. He already weighs more than he's ever weighed, and he's benching more than he's ever benched, squatting more than he's ever squatted. He feels strong. When he looks at himself in his bedroom mirror with his shirt off, though, he can't help but be discouraged. He's thinks he looks a little firmer, but he doesn't look much bigger. His dad tells him not to worry about it, tells him there have been plenty of good backs his size, tells him worrying isn't going to change his body anyway, tells him it might not be the worst thing in the world if the coaches wanted to move him to receiver, or maybe even to the other side of the ball to corner. His mom tells him she hopes that once classes start up, he'll be half as concerned with his studies as he is with his physique. As for Scott, he makes jokes about Gabe's anxiety, uses it to get in digs when he can. When he caught Gabe in front of the mirror yesterday, he shook his head and laughed. "It's not like you're going to Notre Dame, dude. You're trying to walk on at Kutztown. Are you even sure it's football they play there? You sure it's tackle? You sure it's not capture the flag?"

Gabe finishes the last case of cereal and heads to the backroom with the cart of empty boxes. Usually he'd break them down, but these big cereal cases will be good for packing, so he's going to set them aside and take them home. He figures he'll need three or four, and Jeanette says she needs six, but he figures it will be more like eight or ten. She'll leave for State College a couple weeks after Gabe leaves for Kutztown. They'll be about three hours away from each other, so once football season is over, they should be able to spend weekends together. Every other weekend, maybe, depending on how busy they are.

In the back, Gabe stacks the boxes just inside the loading dock door. Outside on the dock, Jugger's smoking a cigarette and drinking straight from a two-liter bottle of 7-Up. He has a clipboard in his hand so if someone important comes by, he can look at it. He has a pen behind his ear.

"Hey," Gabe says. "I'm saving these boxes, so don't break them down."

"For moving?" Jugger says, and he walks slowly toward the store.

"You're a genius," Gabe says.

"Who were those girls I saw you talking to before?" Jugger says. "I like the tall one. You should put in a good word for me."

"She's a decade younger than you," Gabe says.

"I'm young at heart," Jugger says without smiling and turns away from Gabe. "Hey, I was going to ask you, what are you doing Sunday? You only work till noon, right?"

"Well, Jeannette's off Sunday, so we'll probably do something. And

I'll need to get a workout in. And I guess I better start packing one of these days."

Gabe knows what's coming. All summer Jugger's been asking him to hang out. It's not that Gabe doesn't like the guy—he's funny, cool to work with—but he's kind of a burnout, and he's pushing thirty, and there's a desperation in his persistence that makes Gabe uncomfortable. Gabe doesn't feel good about always weaseling out and making excuses, but he doesn't want to hurt Jugger's feelings by just saying no without offering some sort of reason. Jeannette says Gabe should just get it over with and give the poor guy at least one pity date. It would only be right and fair, she says, because of all the pity dates she's given Gabe. A running joke of hers.

"What I was thinking," Jugger says, "is that you could hang out with me and my cousin. We're going to run our bikes over to Centralia. There are some great trails off that section of Route 61 they closed last year. My cousin just got a new bike, and he hasn't sold his old one yet, so you could use that one. It still runs real good." Jugger takes a long pull from his 7-Up and then drops the stub of his cigarette into the bottle. "Little going away party for you. We'll drink some beers and burn some gas. Get you away from the old lady for the afternoon."

"I don't know how to drive a motorcycle," Gabe says. "I never even been on one."

"We'll get you up and running," Jugger says. "You'll love it."

"What do you think my college coach would say about my taking up dirt bikes as a hobby?" Gabe says.

"He isn't your boss yet," Jugger says. "He'd be out of his jurisdiction saying anything."

"You know I lived there when I was a baby?" Gabe says. "In Centralia. Right over the fire, I guess. Jeannette did, too. We didn't even know that about each other until last year."

"Yeah?" Jugger says. "That's something. How things work out."

"Let me check with Jeannette and see what's going on at home this weekend, and then I'll get back to you about Sunday, OK?"

"You always say that," Jugger says. He points a finger at Gabe's chest. "You say you'll get back to me, and then you don't. Whatever. You're not better than me yet, you know. You won't be a college football star for another few weeks. Then, of course, I understand you'll be too good to hang out with me, but now we're still on equal footing. You're just a stock boy at a grocery store. In fact, because of my seniority, I'm kind of your supervisor."

"And don't forget you're a fireman," Gabe says. "You save lives in your spare time. I'm not good enough to hang out with you. And neither's Tammy. That tall girl you saw me talking to earlier. Age difference aside, the real problem is she doesn't deserve you."

"Screw you," Jugger says, and he smirks. "Respect your elders."

PART II

The Prophet, 1969

There are the words, and there are the numbers under the words, and there are the numbers under the numbers. The prophet unburies them and discerns between those that count and those that don't count. The prophet factors the projections and checks them against the patterns. The prophet evens the numbers so they're square. The prophet rounds them up and rounds them down so they figure.

Eleven traps on a trap-line. Minus six, sprung and full. Minus three, unsprung and empty. Minus two, sprung and empty, save for hanks of fur and two clean foreleg bones. Equals coyote. Or equals two coyotes.

Sixty-three headstones in the cemetery—fifty-eight bearing names and seventeen bearing angels and twenty-six bearing crosses—and nine white clouds in the sky. Four buttons on the prophet's shirt. Six buttonholes. Five belt loops on his trousers. Four pockets. Zero empty pockets on account of the knife; and the jerky, six strips; and the flask, four long pulls or seven short pulls; and the other knife.

The fox in the cemetery is. Is still. The groundskeeper found the trap between the thirty-third and thirty-fourth headstones, and he negated it, and when the prophet returned to check it, the groundskeeper told the prophet to stay away. The next night the prophet set another trap, and again the groundskeeper negated it, and when the prophet returned to check it, the groundskeeper called the prophet by the old name, and when the prophet didn't answer, the groundskeeper closed his fist and cuffed the prophet in the ear.

It was one-and-one-half days until the prophet's ear cleared itself. One-and-one-half days of muffled echoes, of tiny bones crackling underwater.

And when the prophet rose from the earth and departed from the place, the groundskeeper tried to follow. For nine steps he tried. And in those nine steps he called the prophet by the old name two more times and asked three questions—"Are you all right?" and "What do you expect?" and "Where are you going?"—and later, after the prophet had returned home and had lain down for the night, it came to pass that the prophet again heard the groundskeeper's voice, now still and small, ask a fourth question: "What shall I do to be saved?"

Three nights later the prophet set the third trap—this time between the eleventh and twelfth headstones—and when the prophet returned to check it, the trap was un-negated by the groundskeeper, and the trap was sprung and full of the groundskeeper's liver-colored cat.

The day of fulfillment draws near.

The prophet can hold his hand over the crevice for seven seconds before he has to pull it back. Before singeing the hair on his arm. The prophet can breathe the crevice's gassy smoke for eleven minutes before he gets sick or goes to sleep.

The crevice is coyote-shaped. The crevice is cat-shaped. The crevice is truth-shaped.

In the beginning there was here as a boy. With his mother and his father and then his other father. In the summer there was the sleeping porch and the heat lightning and the moths and mosquitoes clinging to the screen, and in the winter there was the floor of the living room and the halo of heat and the voice of his mother and his father and then his other father using the old name, telling him to move his blankets back from the stove, to not get too close to the stove.

And then came to pass the cathedral of lies. The misread words and the errant lectures and the unfounded prayers. The prophet learned the truth via the lies. He learned the truth slant-wise, roundabout, outside-in, in spite of. As through a glass darkly. And then the scales fell from his eyes, and he saw the truth words-wise, and he saw the truth numbers-wise. And he kept the truth in his heart, and he pondered it, and he audited it, and he figured it and wrote it, and then the chief priests wanted him to answer for what he had figured and written, and then in their presence he was transfigured, and then in their falsehood-fed fear they cast him out.

And then came to pass the fortress of cross purposes. Only thirteen days and twelve nights. Only the haircut and the boots, the rifle and bunk. Only the weeping and gnashing of teeth. He was only yelled at, and then he was only whispered to. Only a bus ticket and a bus driver who cupped his shoulder and told him not everyone was cut out for it. Only a bus ticket and a bus driver who cupped his shoulder and told him to cut it out or he'd be walking.

Now there is here as a man. Now there is the flask and the trap and the crevice. Now there is what will be.

The crevice is legion. Here it is silent, and there it whistles and hisses.

There it is silent, and here it calls out. Now the fire consumes the bush from the roots up, and then it will uproot the entire harvest. The fire will burn in the land as three hundred foxes, and the fire will burn in the air as the breath of seraphim, and the fire will burn upon the rivers and springs of water like a fallen star, and many people will die of the burning waters, and many will die of the burning air, and many will die of the burning land. And some will die, burning, under the land.

The answerer's voice is even smaller than the questioner's. Even more still. Obey my commandments is how. In precise order and to the nearest whole. Take up your cross is how. Seven times around the perimeter of the city. Knock and seek and ask is how. For water and for bread and for a fish and for an egg. And I shall give you a sponge filled with vinegar. And I shall give you a stone. And I shall give you a serpent. And I shall give you a scorpion.

The thickness of the muskrat's lodge serves to indicate the severity of the previous winter. By a factor of plus or minus seven. The thickness of the muskrat's lodge serves to indicate the severity of the forthcoming winter. By a factor of plus or minus three. Unless there is no forthcoming winter.

The day of fulfillment draws near.

Joanne, 1976

In July, for the bicentennial, I made myself a bonnet and named it Betsy Ross, and I made Philip and Todd three-cornered hats and named them Ben Franklin and Tom Jefferson, and I told Philip and Todd the criminal charge for not wearing Ben and Tom would be treason, and the penalty would be firing squad.

This was three months prior.

We set up across the road from the cemetery to watch the parade. Philip and Todd both were antsy and hot, but they got through it by teasing each other—Philip made fun of Todd's long hair, and Todd made fun of his father's bald spot—and by competing over who could make me laugh hardest. After the parade passed we visited my mother's grave, and then we headed home for steaks, grilled corn, potato salad and beer—Philip let Todd have one but told him not to get used to it—and then we took naps, and then we put our hats back on and drove downtown, to the park, for fireworks. And every single blossom in the sky that night reminded everyone present of the fire under our feet, and every single boom and pop sounded to us like a tick of something counting down, and when the show was over, the sky seemed to all of us blacker than it had been before. As if it had been scorched.

After the show, Todd caught up with some friends and told us he was going to hang out with them for a while. They had a car. And at midnight he still wasn't home, and at one-thirty he still wasn't home, and at two-thirty he still wasn't home. It was after three o'clock when Philip and I finally heard a car in the driveway and then the door. Philip asked me not to, asked me to wait until morning, but I couldn't wait.

Todd was in the kitchen filling a glass at the sink. He was still wearing Tom Jefferson, but backwards, and his hair wasn't in a ponytail anymore, it was hanging loose on his shoulders. I said, "Are you hurt?" and he drank from the glass and then said, "No," and I said, "Are you sorry?" and he took another drink and said, "It wasn't my fault. It was out of my control. But yes, I'm sorry," and then he said, "Is Dad awake?" and I said, "Yes. Your father's awake because he didn't know where his son was at three o'clock in the morning," and he said, "Is he mad or just worried?" and I said, "I'm the one standing here. Maybe I'm the one you should be worried about right now," and he said, "If it were him down here in the kitchen, then you'd be the one I was worrying about." He re-filled his glass, but instead of drinking, he dumped the water slowly into the sink. "I'm tired and don't want to get into it tonight," he said, and I said, "Then go to bed if you're tired. I'm tired, too," and he said, "Then go to bed if you're tired." Then he said, "It really wasn't my fault, but I really am sorry," and I said, "Put yourself in my shoes," and he said, "I know. That's why I'm sorry." I took the glass from his hand and motioned him away from the sink so I could wash it. "Go to bed," I said, and then I said, "I'll wake you up for lunch."

When I returned to the bedroom, Philip was waiting for me. "Well?" he said, and I said, "The little cuss was still wearing his hat," and Philip said, "No firing squad then," and I said, "No firing squad," and Philip said, "Did you tell him to get his hair cut?" and I said, "I neglected to mention that," and then we went to sleep, and we all, the three of us, slept until lunch.

This was three months prior.

Even now my love for my son is whole and simple. Just as it always was. Is my love for my son fuller and deeper than my love for my husband? Is it purer? At any rate, there's not a choice to be made about my love for

Todd. It just is and always was and always will be. Like God. Like God's love. A woman's love for her husband, though, no matter how devout, is human. Its end is always in sight if you take an honest look at it. In a way I suppose this kind of human love is less than, but in another way what makes it less than makes it more than. Not that it should be a contest. But sometimes it is.

When Mom was sick—both when we thought she was just normal sick and then later when we knew she was sick for good, sick in the way we knew she'd never again be well—Philip couldn't have been any better to her. Couldn't have been any better to me. Live with a man long enough, he'll do things and he'll not do things to make you doubt him and question yourself, make you wonder if the turn you'd taken toward him when you were just a girl was a wrong one, but he'll also do and not do other things to make you feel thankful and lucky and wise. I love Philip.

The dreams I had when my mother was dying were informed by fire. I thought of the cancer as burning her up from the inside. One night I remember dreaming that her body grew so hot that the sheets on her hospital bed smoldered, and when I summoned the nurses, they came armed with hoses and buckets of water. Another night I dreamt I was inside her body, a maze of smoky tunnels, and there was no escape. Every path led deeper into the inferno. Eventually I made my way coughing and choking to her heart just in time to watch it ignite. A flaming fist. Finally, on the night before she passed, I dreamt of her funeral and burial. As she was lowered into the ground, the casket burst into flame, and then the whole cemetery, and then the sky was afire, and then the congregation and the minister, and then Philip and Todd and me. Everything joined in fire. Of the three dreams, this is the one I woke up from peacefully. As if it weren't a nightmare.

How Philip responded to these dreams is part of how he was good to me. I'd tell him about them as soon as I woke, and he would sit up with me and hold me, and he wouldn't make to lie down again until I made to lie down again. And the morning after, he wouldn't get up until I got up, and he wouldn't drink the last of the coffee until I made it known I didn't want it, and he'd do the breakfast dishes, and he'd ask me before he left for work if I needed him to stop at the store on the way home, and he'd kiss me twice and tell me what I did with the extra was up to me. I could either keep it for myself or give it away to someone who needed it.

These are the times I now force myself to remember. When I feel bitterness and anger creep into my heart. When it seems easy to imagine my life without Philip, easy to imagine my life as easier without him. When I fool myself into thinking that losing him would help me lose my pain and bring me peace, I remember these moments, and in doing so I'm reminded that there are more important things than peace, and I'm reminded that there's no such thing as easy love, and I'm reminded that loss can't heal loss, that one loss can't be substituted for another, that two losses can't make one loss right.

Philip dreams of Todd, but I don't. I want to and try to—I command myself to dream of him before I fall asleep—but I can't. Where's the justice in that? When Philip shakes and lurches and moans on the other side of the bed, sometimes my instinct is to take his hand in mine or to pull his head into my lap, and other times I feel led to slap his face, and other times I want to leave that bed and go sleep in Todd's room. I don't do anything, though. I just lie there. I just lie. Eyes closed. Pretending to sleep.

I wonder if Sensenig dreams of Todd. I wonder if his scarred and battered heart can take it.

I'd like to dream a dream of Todd that lasted three days, and on the third day I'd like it to end in an open, empty tomb, and there where the boulder had been rolled away, I'd like there to be an angel to say to me, "Do not weep, woman."

Since I can't have Todd in life, and since I can't even dream of him, and since I can't share in Philip's dreams of him, and since I can't even visit his real grave, since the best I can do is visit a marker in the cemetery where I know he isn't, the only thing left is prayer. A poor substitute. Hallowed be thy name. Thy will be done. Give me my daily bread. Forgive me. Thank you for my bread. Thank you for forgiving me. Help me to forgive. Grant me the peace that passeth understanding. No, on second thought, don't grant me that.

Philip doesn't pray. He never has. Not even grace before meals. When my mother was still well, when she still had her house, we'd go there for Thanksgiving, and Philip would keep his eyes open and sneak food to the dog under the table as she recited her long, gratitude-filled blessing. He told me before we got married that he chose not to believe because if he believed he'd have to be angry, and he didn't want to go through life angry. This gave me pause, but then he told me that he liked that I believed, and that maybe through me he'd eventually be able to see his way to something like faith.

A coward's way out, I think now. Left alone in my belief I think this.

Since Todd, the fire has opened up more sinkholes around town. Driveways and streets are buckling. The Garbers, who live behind the American Legion, lost most of their backyard, including the swing set their out-of-town grandchildren played on during visits, and a few blocks away from them, the Trillos lost their vegetable garden. These areas and others have all been fenced off—a chunk of Sensenig's land has been, too, of course, almost three whole acres, including the mine—and officials from this department and that agency have planted Danger and Do Not Trespass signs all along the ridge, but the time for fences and signs is past. This department and that agency have also distributed carbon monoxide detectors to home owners, but the time for detectors has passed. This department and that agency have also drilled holes throughout the town to gauge the temperature and the extent of the fire, but the time for gauging has passed. This department and that agency have also launched investigations into the source of the fire, and they've floated theories about human errors like smoldering trash fires at the town landfill and acts of God like lightning strikes, but the time for investigations and theories has passed. The hunters say the woods are peppered here and there with swallowed-up trees and hillside cave-ins, and the fishermen say there are places along the creek where you can hear the rocks sizzle when it rains. On some days, depending on the direction of the wind, the fumes and smoke are powerful enough to make you cough. You have to shut your windows and wait it out. The fire will eventually eat the town down to nothing. Like crows on carrion.

So three losses to mourn. The mother, the son and the smoldering town. Lined up like so. Like crosses on a hillside. Like dark birds on the shoulder of the road.

And we. Philip and I. The two of us. We have half a new roof.

Vonda, 1984

When I first started working for Sy, we'd get calls everyday about the fire. As soon as the state started to pay for people to relocate and to buy their homes so they could be razed, the phone didn't stop ringing. People wanting to bring litigation against the state, the town, the mining companies. They smelled a little money, and they wanted more. Even the mining companies themselves would check in now and then to inquire about retaining Sy's services. Sy figured this reflected strategy more than need on their part. They had plenty of their own lawyers. The only reason they were looking to employ the small-time law offices in the area was because they thought this would be a way to cut down on the number of lawsuits filed against them. The more lawyers they retained, the fewer there would be available to the people who wanted to get into their pockets.

No matter who called, though, if it were about the fire, Sy wasn't interested. He said no to all comers. When I asked him why, he told me that no matter how he chose, he'd have people mad at him who he didn't want mad at him; and he said this kind of litigation is the kind that drags on for decades, and he didn't know if he had the necessary attention span for work like that; and he said, when it came down to it, he had always been a bit lazy, from the time he was a boy, never very ambitious, and, frankly, the whole fire situation sounded like it could be a lot of work for a lawyer.

Sy made all his jokes straight-faced. On top of that, sometimes when he was serious, his mouth would curve into a smirk. It took me a little while to get used to this.

He never said so, but during my time with Sy, I grew to believe that the real reason he didn't get involved with litigating the fire was because he didn't know who was in the wrong—he didn't know who should be held most accountable—and he didn't want to place blame where it shouldn't be placed. On the basis of this theory, I formulated another. I decided that a man who took care not to be wrong in assigning blame was likely a man who took care not to do wrong, and a man who took care not to do wrong was likely a good man. As backwards as it sounds, what happened between Sy and me, the wrong we did, never would have happened if I hadn't decided he was a good man.

Those first few times—when we still thought we would stop, when we still thought we could—whenever we'd finish, one of us would say something like, "Where is this coming from?" or "What is this all about?" We didn't say it like we were unhappy or like we felt guilty, but we didn't say it in celebration, either; rather, it was as if we were trying to convince ourselves that what was moving us was something mysterious, something beyond us that we had yet to figure out. I think turning it into a riddle was a stall tactic.

For the time being, it allowed us to deny knowing what we very well knew. The reason we turned it into a mystery was the same reason I never said, "Chuck," and he never said, "Beth."

Eventually Sy and I started to worry about being together in the office. Even though we were almost always alone, we were worried that it looked suspicious locking the door in the middle of the day, leaving the phones go unanswered, drawing the shades up and down. So we started seeing each other outside the office. We'd leave for lunch or at the end of the day in our separate cars—he'd usually give me a ten-minute head start—and then we'd meet somewhere. When it was raining, we'd head to one of the old mining roads and stay in one of our cars. If it were nice, we'd head to the woods. Sy knew spots. My favorite was underneath his deer stand.

The last time was there. We told each other that it would be the last time until we both came clean with our spouses. They were people we cared about, people we'd had pleasant histories with, people whom, at one time, we'd felt passionate about. Maybe at one time we'd even felt as passionate about these people as we did at present about each other. "Would you want to know, or would you want to be lied to? Even though it would be painful, wouldn't you want to know?" Sy asked me. I told him I would. I would want to know rather than be lied to. But I'm not sure I said so because it was the truth or because agreeing is easier. It's almost always easier.

The next morning, a Saturday, I got out of bed and set up outside on the back deck. I brought a cup of tea with me and waited for Chuck. I thought for some reason it would go better outside. The fresh air. Things would seem less dire maybe. The open sky. Maybe we'd feel less like everything was closing in on us. And we'd never made love on the back deck, and as far as I could remember, we'd never argued on the back deck, and with fall coming on, it seemed like the right place to discuss the end of something. I was thinking along these lines at that time in my life. Like the world held meanings for those who were interested. This means that. How people in love think.

The view from the deck was gorgeous. We had a maple tree in the backyard, and its shady side had turned yellow, and its sunny side had turned red, and the last of the squash in our garden was over-ripe and rotting sweetly in the frost-tinged mud, and the early sky looked backlit, like a sheet with a flashlight behind it. If I were to leave, I thought, I'd miss all this. I'd miss the house, the deck, the backyard. I didn't know if I'd be the one leaving or not, though. Maybe Chuck would want to be the one to leave. Leave first. The likelihood was that neither of us would be allowed to stay for long. The state kept expanding the area they wanted evacuated, and our number would come up sooner or later. At any rate, I'd leave all that up to Chuck. Whatever he thought. Whatever he wanted. And I wouldn't ask him for anything. Working in law offices, I'd seen the ugly things couples do and say to each other in parting. Even with some of the ones who stay civil for the most part, you can catch glimpses of the anger. You can hear it in what they don't say. Sitting out there on the deck that morning, I told myself I'd be different. I was going to be gracious and patient. I was going to do my best to love Chuck through this. This is what I was telling myself. Even though I'd be at the root of Chuck's pain, who's to say that I couldn't somehow also be a source of support and comfort? Kumbaya and come together. This is how I was trying to get my mind to work that morning. I was making myself think along these lines so I wouldn't feel guilty about how I wasn't feeling guilty.

"You going to stay out here? It's cold out here," Chuck said. I turned in my chair to see him. Shirtless, munching toast. The sliding glass door was open behind him. "Aren't you planning on going to work today? Don't tell me Sy's given you a Saturday off?"

"Can you come sit?" I said. "We need to talk."

"Talk inside," he said. "I'm losing the feeling in my extremities."

"I'd rather you come out here," I said. "Grab a jacket."

Chuck disappeared for a few minutes, and when he came back he was fully dressed. He was even wearing shoes and a cap. "Today's the day, huh?" he said.

"What's that mean?" I said. "Today's the day for what?"

"You tell me," Chuck said. "Be a big girl. This isn't something I'm going to do for you."

So I told him what he already knew. What he already had an inkling of, anyway. He had questions he needed answered to fill in the blanks, though. He wanted to know how long, how many times, and if the baby was why. I told him almost seven months, a lot of times, and I don't know why. It was like court testimony with just the witness and lawyer. Without the jury and judge.

The last thing Chuck wanted to know was who started it. This was a question that Sy and I playfully argued about sometimes. Who was the seducer and who was the seducee. Who was the spark and who was the tinder. "We both started it," I said. "And we both tried to stop it, and we both kept it going instead."

"Something neither of you could resist. Like animal magnetism. You couldn't deprive yourself of each other. His paunch. His turkey neck. How could you be expected to be true to your husband?"

"Every mean thing you say I deserve," I said. "I know this isn't fair. I know it's selfish."

"Your knowing doesn't make it better," Chuck said. "It makes it worse." Up to this point his tone had been even, and he'd been looking to the ground or to the side when he spoke. This was the first thing he yelled, and it was the first thing he said while looking me in the eye. He stood, stepped off the deck and took a few steps into the yard. It was like he wanted to get further away from me. For my good. For his own good. His steps made faint footprints in the long, damp grass. "Confessing this to me doesn't make anything better if it's something you're going to keep doing," he said. "And you're telling me it's something you're going to keep doing, right?"

I didn't say anything. I nodded.

"I guess I have a lawyer I need to see," Chuck said. That was it then. He took a right, turned the corner of the house, and headed up the hill toward the front yard. I heard the garage door open, and then I heard his car leave.

When Sy answered the phone at the office, I told him Chuck was on his way over. "I don't know what's on his mind," I said.

"You told him?" Sy said.

"Like we talked about," I said. "I think he already kind of knew. I don't know if that made it worse or better."

"I couldn't tell Beth," Sy said. "I didn't yet, I mean."

"Oh," I said.

"I will, though, Vonda. I will today. I'll wait for Chuck and deal with that, and then I'll go home and tell Beth."

"Oh," I said. "You'll wait for Chuck?"

"I'll take what's coming," he said. "Get it over with. And then when Beth gets home tonight, I'll tell her. Get that over with. She's in State College for homecoming. If it gets to be too late, I'll tell her tomorrow morning. First thing."

"Oh," I said again. "OK."

"Vonda," he said.

"When will I see you?" I said.

Jeanette, 1995

We were careful most of the time. We were more than we weren't. So it's not fair. I know at least three friends of mine who would love if this were happening to them, but it's not happening to them, it's happening to me, and I would do anything for it not to be happening. So it's not fair at all. That something should happen to someone who doesn't want it to happen, to someone who tried to be careful most of the time, while it could just as easily happen to someone who does want it. Someone who wasn't as careful or someone who would be totally fine with it.

I don't know which time it was, but if I did, I would give up that whole day of my life if it could be fixed that way. If I could make it unhappen that way. Even if it couldn't be narrowed down to one day. I'd give up a whole week. I'd give up a month. That time we broke up early last fall, when I was getting sick of coming in third behind football and his friends, I'd go back in time to make that breakup stick if doing so would make this unhappen.

We were apart almost two weeks that time. Then he showed up at my house on a Sunday morning when my parents were at church. He had already been seated in a pew with his parents when he saw mine come in without me. He got right up and left, took his parents' car. Without even asking. Like a movie. I made him ring the doorbell six times before I let him in. The last two times he rang it we were looking at each other through the window. Those last two times were like him saying please. If I had to do it over, if doing it over could stop what's happened from happening, I would just not open the door. Or I'd let him in and hear him out, but I would be firm about not getting back together, about just being friends. Or I'd get back together with him for a little while so we'd be able go to the prom and the senior dinner dance the next fall. The dinner dance was better than the prom. We had it on a boat, on the Susquehanna, and the music was better, and there was less drama because we were more mature as seniors than we were as juniors, and there wasn't the hassle of choosing a queen and king, and there wasn't the hassle of tuxes and gowns. It was only about cherishing each other, cherishing the moment. I'd break up with Gabe right after that. Right after we stepped off the boat. Or right when summer started. We hardly saw each other anyway with us both working and him working out all the time. Working out for nothing it turned out. We obviously saw each other some—this wouldn't be happening if we didn't—but the time we had together was always rushed, and he was always tired. I could have just used that as a reason for breaking up. If we couldn't seem to make time for each other when we were living in the same town, how were we going to do it when we were living in different towns, going to different colleges?

I wouldn't have been able to stop loving Gabe, not right away, but if it meant this not happening, I could have learned. I could've figured out how to stop.

But what's happening is happening. My mom tells me I need to get this through my head. For a while she was really tender with me. It reminded me of how she was when I was little. The night I told her, she just held me on the couch like she used to when I'd stay home sick from elementary school. And for a couple weeks after, she'd just come up to me out of the blue and give me a hug. Then we told my dad, and things shifted. He didn't get mad like I thought he might. He just got quiet and sad, like what was happening to me was happening to him. I thought it was selfish how he was acting, like he was the one I should feel sorry for rather than the other way around, and now my mom's done this complete switch. She's on me like she never has been before. "You have four months to do a lot of growing up," she told me the other day. She was mad my room was a mess and that I'd forgotten to switch the laundry. This is the kind of stuff she used to get irritated at me about, but it's like now, with me being pregnant, she has this new ammunition that allows her to get angrier. Before, almost always, especially if my dad was around, arguments about housework and me being a slob would be kind of no big deal. My dad might even pipe up with a joke. Sometimes he told my mom that she had to take into account that I was a Centralia baby, that I really wasn't doing that bad as a member of society if you took into account the fact that noxious fumes had probably eaten away most of my brain before I was even a toddler. Mom wouldn't laugh, and I wouldn't either, but we'd stop snipping at each other, which was my dad's whole intent for making the joke in the first place. To keep the peace.

The plan for now is for me to stay put. I'm in limbo. The baby will be here in four months, in March, and the two of us, the baby and I, will hang out at my parents'. One step at a time. That's what everyone's saying to me. Even Gabe's saying it.

It was only a few weeks before he was supposed to leave for football camp when I told him. I told my mom a week before that, and she asked if I'd told Gabe yet, and I said I hadn't, and she hugged me and told me that I needed to, but that I'd be on my own timetable. That it was up to me when.

By the end of the week, though, she was telling me the sooner the better, that he had a right to know. So much for my timetable. "None of this has been on my own timetable," I said to her, and she told me to pull myself together, that having a pity party wasn't going to help anyone. Leastways my baby. She said this a week in.

I borrowed my mom's car and drove to Weis's at the end of the Gabe's shift. I found his car in the lot and parked right next to it and waited. He came out with that guy he works with. Jugger. Now his new best friend, I guess, although at the time Gabe was always complaining to me that the guy was getting on his nerves. When they saw me, Jugger punched Gabe in the arm and said something not quite loud enough for me to hear, but I can imagine the kind of comment it was, either something about me being a ball and chain, like because of me Gabe can't have any fun, or something about me and sex. A lot of times you don't have to hear what guys say to each other to know what they're saying. Bad enough when it's guys your own age, but when it's someone older like Jugger, it's grosser. And it's more disappointing. Like evidence that boys don't ever really change that much.

"What's up?" Gabe said. He leaned into the open driver's side window to kiss me. I couldn't lift my face up—I wanted to look at him, but I couldn't—so he kissed the top of my head. "What's the matter?" he said. "Did I do something?"

"Can you get in?" I said.

I didn't want to have the conversation in the parking lot of a grocery store, so I drove us to the river, to the state park up near Sunbury. The drive took thirty minutes or so, and although we didn't say much, I could tell he was half-worried about what was on my mind, and half-irritated that I was messing with his workout schedule.

At the park, I took Gabe's hand and led him down to the water, and then he led me over to a bench and we sat. "Here we are," he said. "Fake Lake Park."

"Why Fake Lake?" I said.

"That's what my dad calls it. Because of the inflatable dam. They call this Augusta Lake in the summer, but come fall, they deflate the dam, and it goes back to being the plain old Susquehanna River again."

"I know how it works," I said. "I'm from around here, remember?"

"You asked," he said.

"I meant why do you call it 'Fake Lake'? It's not fake. It's just temporary. It comes and goes."

"Real lakes don't come and go," he said, and he pressed the heels of his hands into his eyes. Like talking to me was a painful ordeal. "Why are we here?" he said.

"I'm pregnant is why," I said. "My mom made me a doctor's appointment for Monday morning. Want to come?"

Gabe later told me that I sounded mad when I said this. Bitter. But I wasn't bitter. I wasn't just mad and bitter. I don't know what I was.

Gabe looked at me for a long time before I turned to look at him, and then as soon as I did, he looked at the water. "So you're keeping it then?" Gabe said. "That kind of doctor's appointment? Or the other kind?"

"My mom knows, Gabe. I didn't know what to do, so I told her. So yeah, I'm keeping it. My mom knows, so it's too late to not keep it. So yeah. Even if my mom didn't know, I don't think I could do that. I don't think I could not keep it."

"OK," Gabe said.

"It's really hot, right?" I said. "Isn't it really hot?"

"We should get you out of the heat," Gabe said, but neither of us moved right away.

"I'm going to get fat," I said. "I don't know how to be fat."

"You'll only be fat for a while," Gabe said, "and then when the baby comes, you won't be fat."

"I'll deflate like the dam," I said. "Like the damn dam."

"We'll be OK," he said.

"We will," I said. "We will be OK."

"We will," he said.

PART III

The Prophet, 1969

How things wind down, how they regress.

The prophet will fold himself closed. Like a finished book. He'll close himself so he can be re-opened. Like a lost scroll found. He'll roll himself into the crevice. Too close. Like a map following itself. Rendered faithfully and drawn to scale. Closer still.

The first snow is when.

The prophet welcomes the cup. The cup is the will of the truth, and it is his will. He will not cry out, and he will not forsake nor be forsaken, and he will not ask that they be forgiven, and he will not ask for the cup to be removed from him. Rather, he will bring it to his lips and drink. Four long pulls or seven short pulls.

The prophet can breathe the crevice's smoke for eleven minutes before he goes to sleep. The breadth of the crevice and the length of the crevice and the height of the crevice and the depth of the crevice. The prophet will breathe them one at a time, and then he will descend, and then he will breathe them all at once, and then he will be breathed.

Through the bare crowns of trees, the prophet watches the dusk-grey, bottom-heavy sky, and he watches his breath rise like frozen smoke. He swings the groundskeeper's pickaxe over his right shoulder, and he swings it over his left shoulder. For when the groundskeeper came upon the prophet in the groundskeeper's shed, the groundskeeper asked, "Why are you taking that?" and he asked, "Do you need to borrow it?" and he called the prophet by the old name and said, "If I let you borrow it, will you return it?" And the prophet swung the pickaxe over his right shoulder, and he swung it over his left shoulder.

The prophet opens up the crevice. The prophet opens up the crevice to be groundskeeper-shaped, and the prophet opens up the crevice to be prophet-shaped. And a chip of rock leaps up to bite the prophet in the chest, and a chip leaps up to bite him in the neck, and a chip leaps up to bite him in the head, and blood trickles down from the crevice in his head to the crevice of his eye like sweat, and blood trickles down from the crevice of his eye into the crevice of the crevice like tears, and there is in this a work completed, and there is in this a promise kept, and there is in this the truth echoed, and there is in this the truth prefigured.

And the snow shall fall into the prophet's blood-filled, sightless crevice like light. And the snow shall fall into the prophet's hungry, silent crevice like manna. And the snow shall fall into the crevice of the crevice, preparing the way for the prophet, who is preparing the way.

And it shall come to pass that the lion's mouth will not be shut, and it shall come to pass that the furnace's flames will not be cooled, and it shall come to pass that there will not be sent a comforter.

When the prophet lays his body down to be broken in the crevice, and when he eats the smoke and drinks the fire in remembrance of himself, then it shall come to pass that the flask will be filled by its own emptiness, and the crow will pluck its own feather and shriek at the loss, and the muskrat will resurface and choke on the thickness of the air, and the fox will be singed by the torch of its own tail, and the turkey buzzard will glide high in slow, eternal, retrograde circles around the ghosts of its own slow, eternal, retrograde circles.

The day of fulfillment draws nearer. Nearer still.

Sensenig, 1976

When I had my first eight years ago, they told me to take it easy. Told me not to exert myself. Told me to start acting my age. In the wake of this one, though, they're telling me to take brisk walks. To buy a pair of sneakers. One of the doctors who came to my room put down his clipboard to take Muriel's hand in his—he thought he was charming—and told her she should get me to take her dancing twice a week. Another doctor, the one who signed my papers on my way out, said, "Calisthenics." They say there have been new studies done over the last decade, and these new ones trump the old ones. You think about it, though, who's to say today's doctors know better than yesterday's? They just think they do. It'll be the same with tomorrow's doctors. They'll overcompensate for the past, call it progress and laugh all the way to the bank. And all around them their patients will continue to drop dead with heart attacks and strokes just like they always have. Things wear out eventually. Arteries and muscles and organs included. There are no real fixes. Try to get a doctor to admit that to you, though.

I shouldn't have let Philip bring his boy with him. It's not boy's work. At one time it was. When I was a boy it was boy's work. But it's not work for boys who are boys now. Boys were made into men before they were ready back then, and now boys aren't made into men until sometimes it's too late. Sometimes never. It's not just doctors who overcompensate for history.

This to say, Philip's boy wasn't a man. He shouldn't have been doing the work. I'm an old man. I shouldn't have been doing the work. And Philip's a house painter. Three people in a place where they had no business being, doing work they had no business doing.

I was a boy when the pit was dug. Just old enough to remember. More than a few folks around had their own pits back then. People call them bootleg pits, but they didn't start calling them that until the '20s or '30s. After whiskey bootlegging. My pit pre-dates all that. Besides, these little family coal holes weren't illegal. Not so much, anyway. The companies knew about them. If a guy started shopping his coal around and making a real operation out of it he might get a talking to, but most just dug enough for their own stoves. Maybe a neighbor or two. Wasn't worth it for the companies to give these folks a hard time.

I wasn't but nine or ten the first time they cranked me down into the hole. My dad and his brothers were done for the day. This was just for fun. That's what they were they thinking. I kept pestering them about wanting to do it, about how I was big and strong enough, so they thought they'd throw me down there for a few minutes to show me what I was asking for. Scare me quiet. Take me down a notch. When I yelled up and they hoisted me to the surface, I remember smiling at their surprised voices as I rode through the dark. I'd lasted a good bit longer than they thought I would, and the cart was heavier than they thought it would be.

They couldn't believe it when they saw I'd filled almost half. My uncles lifted me out and commenced mussing my hair and slapping my back. I remember one of them in particular, my Uncle Reuben, squeezing my biceps and calling me Samson. My pop, though, hung back. Of course he did. He shoveled the coal I'd dug out of the cart and into the truck, and on the way home he let me steer a little on the straightaways like he usually did, and like usual he didn't say much, but I sensed he was proud, even if reluctantly so, even if he was doing all he could to try to hide his pride from me. Back then you took care not to over-praise your children. Your sons especially. For their own good you took care. The world's a hard place, harder still if you go through thinking you're more than you are. Nowadays, every kid's a genius. Go to a little league game and listen to the hubbub in the bleachers. Every boy's Johnny Bench. People overcompensate.

This last time at the pit was to be the last time. I said that going in. Even before what happened with Philip's boy I'd made that decision. I'd already bought and installed the new oil furnace Muriel wanted, and I'd already told my handful of customers that my next delivery to them would be the last. None of them argued with me or seemed worried. Arguing and worrying are for younger people, and none of my customers were young. Clifford Payne asked me why, though. That's the most response I got. When I answered him—I told him I was too old—he said, "If you're too old, what does that make me?" and we had a laugh. Clifford will be fine. He's surrounded by family out there in Byrnesville, and his house is tiny enough he could heat the whole thing with wood or kerosene.

At first Philip wouldn't let the boy into the pit. He and I took turns in the cart, and the boy stayed on the surface and helped crank us up and down. He wasn't a strong boy. When it was me and him on the crank, it was a struggle to pull his dad out of the pit. That's what got me straining and overdoing it. Not so much my turns in the hole swinging the pick, but my turns up top, cranking the cart.

Besides being soft-muscled, the boy didn't make for very good company either. When his dad was in the pit, the boy just paced the bank, threw rocks—he kind of led with his elbow like Muriel does when she tries to throw—and now and then it looked like he was pretending to play the guitar, pretending to play the drums. He fancied himself a one-man band, I guess. When I took out my pipe he perked up a little bit—he strolled over and asked me where I got it—but other than that we were pretty quiet with each other. I don't think he liked it when I asked him why the hell he had a ponytail. He didn't know what to say. I think he was pouting the whole time. He didn't like me asking about his ponytail, and he didn't like his dad not letting him take turns in the hole.

Then Philip gave in to his son. I don't know what the boy said to get his father to change his mind—whatever was said was said when I was in the pit—but I had mixed feelings about it. On the one hand, I think the boy should've been taking his turns in the cart all along, but on the other hand, I felt ashamed for Philip that he didn't stand his ground. That's not how to rear a boy. You can't allow him to get the idea that your rules and decisions are up for negotiation. I stayed out of it, though. It was my pit, but it wasn't my son.

I'm not making to blame Philip for what happened. It doesn't make sense to try to assign blame for what happened. To do so makes the cruelness of what happened even more cruel. There's going to be grief to deal with. You can't deal with it, though, by overcompensating. Pointing a finger. Now you're not only grieving, you're also bitter. So you've made it worse by half. And you haven't made anything better. The boy's still dead.

I remember helping the boy get situated in the cart, and I remember his father giving him instructions, and I remember that after each instruction the boy would say, "I know, I know" even though he didn't know—how could he know?—and every time he said it I felt like cuffing him in the ear. Rather, I felt like I wanted Philip to cuff him in the ear. Then I remember Philip and me cranking him down, and when we were done cranking, I remember thinking maybe I'd pulled or pinched something up into my shoulder. Then it felt like all the muscles in my chest were being squeezed together, like a bear had maybe snuck up behind me, and my head began to swim, and I dropped to my knees.

Philip told me to hang on, and he yelled down into the pit to the boy and started to crank him up, and then I heard it. The pit caving in on itself. It wasn't a terribly loud sound. It was low and rumbling, like distant thunder, but the approaching storm was under your feet instead of over your head. The last thing I remember seeing was the free end of the crank cable whip up into the air like snapped fishing line, and the last thing I remember hearing was Philip screaming, and the last thing I remember feeling was him hoisting me up into his arms. One arm under my knees and one under my neck. Like I was a child.

Philip carried me to his truck and drove me the half-mile down to the house and screamed for Muriel to call an ambulance for me and to call for help for his boy, and then he was back in the truck and gone again. This I know from Muriel. She says he dumped me on the kitchen floor like I was a sack of something.

"He left his boy," I said.

"The boy was already gone," Muriel said. "Philip did the right thing. I'm thankful for that."

When the cops and the fire truck got to the mine, they say Philip was waist deep in the rubble. Took four men to get him out of there, and as soon as they did, the collapse collapsed. New rubble on top of old rubble. And then that layer collapsed. Later that afternoon, when they were still talking about what to do, the whole mess collapsed again. And then they stopped even talking about any kind of effort to get to the boy.

Since then, the crews who have come by have theories. They dug holes all around the site, sunk their gauges into the earth, and came up with the fire as the culprit. They didn't know it had spread this far, in this direction. One of them came to the house to talk to me. He compared the fire they're dealing with here to a forest fire. "A forest fires has a mind of its own," he said. "You can draw up all the models you want, but there's no telling how it will bob and weave. That's part of what makes fighting it so difficult. A forest fire, though, despite its unpredictability, at least you can see it." This fellow had a wardrobe I found curious. He wore a hard hat, but also a tie. His hands were clean and manicured—they reminded me of a doctor's hands—but he wore work boots. "Mine fires like this are even tougher than forest fires," he said. "In terms of analyzing them and reining them in. There are more variables. And we don't know everywhere it is, and we don't know how deep or shallow it's burning, and we don't know the kind of damage it's doing. And these are just the unknowns that we know about. One thing's clear, though. You all need to get out of here."

On top of all this, he tells me he shouldn't be saying what he's saying. He tells me that sharing what he's sharing with me is jumping the gun, and that jumping the gun could get him in trouble, but he says he wouldn't be able to sleep at night if he didn't tell me. At that point in the conversation I wanted to tell him he didn't know the first thing about not sleeping at night. I wanted to tell him to add that to his long list of things he didn't know the first thing about.

For a while after what happened there was talk floating around about Philip and his wife suing me because that's the world we live in, and I did end up getting a call from Sy Silvernell, a lawyer in town, and he came out to the house to talk, and later on that same week he called and asked if I'd be willing to write a check to reimburse Philip and his wife for the boy's funeral arrangements, and I said of course I would, but then a few days after that he called me back to tell me to forget it. Philip and his wife had decided they didn't want that from me. They'd decided they didn't want anything. Hearing this made me want to write the biggest check I'd ever written. I told Muriel that I needed to call them, but she wouldn't let me. I got worked up over that. Her not letting me. I got exercised over that and started feeling some twinges in my chest. Muriel sat me down, gave me a glass of water and a nitroglycerin, and told me nothing good would come of me calling. She said they needed time and space and that grief can be a hard thing to sort out and that sometimes it never gets sorted out. She told me calling them would be selfish.

She's right, of course, that calling wasn't the right thing to do, and I was right to listen to her—I've spent my life listening to Muriel, and I've been served well in doing so—but I wish there were a way for the boy's mother to understand that I was just trying to be neighborly in asking her husband to help me out in the pit. I knew from Zuccari that he had just talked her and Philip into a new roof, and I figured they could use the money. Her knowing this would not help her one goddam bit, but I still want her to know. And I want her to know that I didn't ask Philip to leave his boy while he drove me to my house. I would have never asked him to do that. To leave his boy behind. Even if the boy was already gone, I wouldn't have asked that.

Is Muriel right that it's out of selfishness I want Philip's wife to know this? I want her to know this so that I can feel better? It wouldn't work that way anyway. I wouldn't feel better. It would make me feel worse because of how I suspect myself of selfishness. Still. I want her to know.

She never will know, though. She never will because I'm listening to Muriel. I'm taking walks with Muriel at night, and I'm taking the pills she gives me that the doctors have given her, and I'm taking her hints about Florida. It seems to be the only thing on her mind all of a sudden—I think she's overcompensating a bit, trying hard to fool herself happy—but my son and daughters are encouraging her in that direction, and I can see why they'd want to. So. It looks like Muriel and me are going to end up down south sometime in the next while. Retirement brochures all over our house. Pictures of golfers and shuffleboarders and beachwalkers. Muriel's double-checked, and I've got doctor's clearance for all of it.

Chuck, 1984

It was already in the glove compartment. Had been there for a month. Prior to that it had sat in the attic for more than a decade, since Chuck's father had passed and his things had been left to Chuck to deal with. At one point there used to be a shoulder holster that went with the pistol—Chuck remembered using it for his cap guns as a boy—but it had been lost long ago. In the woods somewhere. Chuck remembered being nervous to tell his father he'd lost it, and then being surprised and grateful and a bit confused when his father hadn't seemed irritated at all.

Chuck would see the gun a few times a year. When it came time to get out or put away the camping gear or install or take out the storm windows or set up or tear down the artificial Christmas tree—Vonda was allergic to the real thing—he'd see it wrapped in an oilcloth between Vonda's old sewing machine and the disassembled crib, but he wouldn't think, "Gun," he'd think, "Dad." This last time, though, over the long July 4th weekend, when he was up in the attic laying insulation, he saw it and thought, "Gun," and he picked it up and held it for a while, and later that day he stopped by the sporting goods store for oil and ammunition, and he cleaned it up and loaded it.

Chuck hadn't been planning to insulate the attic over the holiday weekend. He'd wanted to get away to Philly with Vonda for a couple nights, maybe see a ball game like they used to. It looked like it was going to be the Mets' year, but Schmidt was having a good season, on his way to another MVP award it would turn out, and Chuck thought it would do Vonda and him some good to get out of town, sit together in a crowd, share an expensive beer—she never wanted her own, only wanted to sip off his—and then have dinner somewhere new, at a place they'd never been before. Something you can do in a city.

Vonda, though, told him she couldn't because of work. Things were hectic at the office, and Sy needed her. He would pay her time-and-a-half, of course, for working the weekend, so it would be worth it. "We can't all have cushy government jobs," Vonda said. She said it playfully, but it irritated Chuck just the same, and it irritated him, too, that she encouraged him to go to Philly on his own. So he decided he had to insulate the attic. He couldn't go to Philly for the weekend because he had to spend time and money insulating the attic of a house they both knew they'd probably have to leave behind sooner rather than later, and he had to do this in July, in the middle of a heat wave, with the daytime temperatures in the mid-90s. "Is this you pouting?" Vonda had asked.

After cleaning the gun, Chuck put it in his sock drawer for a week, where he saw it every morning—if Vonda noticed it there in the dresser when putting away laundry, she never said anything—and then he moved it out to the garage, to the bottom of his tool box, and told himself to forget about it. Eventually, though, it found its way into his car.

Chuck didn't know all the details, and he didn't know the extent of what was going on—he couldn't say under oath that he was absolutely sure of anything—but he'd suspected something was happening between Vonda and Sy. When Vonda seemed to turn a corner of sorts this past spring— since they'd lost the baby three years ago, this was the most lighthearted and happiest she'd been—Chuck was relieved and encouraged at first, but the longer her happiness went on, the more he felt excluded from it. The more he felt like it had nothing to do with him. Like it had no room for him. One day he'd feel stupid and paranoid, and then he'd feel stupid and angry, and then he'd feel stupid and ashamed, and then he'd feel stupid and humiliated. A few times he wanted to ask Vonda straight out, but he had a feeling that as soon as he said anything, as soon as the words were out of his mouth, he would realize how wrong and unfair they were, and there would be no taking them back.

Before the gun came out of the glove compartment in front of Sy Silvernell's office, it had come out once before. In early September, on his commute to Harrisburg one early morning—Chuck pushed paper at the Department of Transportation—he clipped a woodchuck out on Fairgrounds Road. When Chuck saw in the rearview mirror that the animal was still alive and wriggling, he pulled a U-turn, grabbed the pistol, scanned the empty road for headlights, and put the thing out of its misery. He then raised the pistol, took approximate aim at the dark clump of trees halfway up the bank on the road's shoulder, and squeezed the trigger twice. When he got back in the car and returned the warm gun to the glove compartment, his heart was beating fast and heavy enough that he could see his shirt moving.

A month later, when Chuck pulled up to the curb in front of Sy's office, he got out of the car without the gun, but after trying the front door and finding it locked, and then banging on it and not getting an answer, Chuck surprised himself by heading back to the car, and then he was surprised by the pistol in his hand, and for the rest of the morning he never stopped being surprised.

Chuck was halfway up the walk on his return to the door when Sy opened it and stepped onto the small porch. Chuck raised the pistol, flat against his chest, and with his other hand waved Sy down the stairs. "Let's get in the car," he said, and Sy said, "Chuck?" and he looked around, like he was searching for someone, but there was no one else. The streets and sidewalks were empty. There weren't even any birds in the sky. "What are we up to here?" he said, and Chuck said, "I don't know, Sy. What are we up to?" and then they walked to the car, and Chuck opened the passenger side door, and Sy climbed in, and then Chuck said, "No, wait. You're driving," and Sy got out of the car and circled around to the other door and let himself in. "Your hands," Chuck said from the sidewalk. "Ten and two on the steering wheel." When Sy obliged, Chuck seated himself and gave Sy the keys.

"Where are we going?" Sy said, and Chuck said, "I don't know. Where should we go? How about this. How about you take me where you take her," and Sy said, "There are a few places. Which one?" and Chuck said, "Right. A few places. How about this. How about you take me to the best one," and Sy said, "You sure this is how it needs to go?" and Chuck said, "Take me to her favorite place," and Sy said, "Her favorite place is right here. Right here at the office," and Chuck said, "Take me to her second favorite place," and Sy said, "I'd rather not, Chuck. I don't think that would be a good idea for either of us," and Chuck said, "No, you're right. It's a horrible idea, but that's what we're doing this morning, horrible things," and Sy said, "I'll be honest with you, Chuck. It's in the woods. Up above the cemetery a ways. I have a deer stand out there. This is me being up front with you. I think we're both better off here, though. We're better off talking here in the car or going into the office and talking," and Chuck said, "You're right. We would be better off staying here. But that's not what we're going to do. We're not going to do the better thing. We're going to your deer stand. Would you please drive me to your deer stand? Given all that's happened, could you see your way clear to do this one goddam thing for me?" and Sy said, "All right, Chuck. I'll do it. I'll drive you there because I trust you, because I trust you're not going to do anything that you can't take back," and Chuck said, "You'll drive me there because I'm pointing a gun at you is why you'll drive me there," and Sy put on the blinker, checked both mirrors, and pulled out into the street.

On the way out of town, the men were quiet. At one point, Chuck almost said, "See what you've done?" and then he almost said, "Let's swing by the house and pick up Vonda," and then he almost said, "Stop the car and get out and stay far away from me," but he didn't say any of these things. Only Sy spoke, once, asking if there were a pair of sunglasses somewhere he could use, and Chuck answered that there wasn't, even though he knew there was. In the glove compartment.

After about ten minutes Sy turned off onto an old mining road and said, "We're just a couple miles away," and then he slowed the car down to a crawl and steered carefully around the divots in the road. After a little while he pulled over and said, "We're here," and he pointed out Chuck's window. "That trail there leads to the deer stand."

Chuck opened his door and said, "Let's go."

Chuck walked behind Sy on the muddy, narrow trail for a good while until Sy finally stopped under a black walnut tree, turned to face Sy, and pointed up. "That's my deer stand up there," he said. "So here we are. Now what?" he said. "Now what, Chuck?"

"Vonda's been up there?" Chuck said, looking up and shielding his eyes with the pistol.

"You think we wanted this to happen?" Sy said. He bent over to pick up a twig, and when he straightened, he snapped it in his fingers. "You think either Vonda or I wanted to make a mess of things like this?"

"I asked if Vonda's been up there with you," Chuck said.

"She got up there once," Sy said. "She didn't like it, though, so we came down right away. She likes this spot here, though. This clearing."

"She doesn't like heights," Chuck said, and then he looked at the ground. "So you spread out a blanket, I guess. You clear away all the walnuts so the ground is nice and smooth, and then you roll out your blanket or your tarp or whatever, and then you get to it."

"Are you going to kill me, Chuck?" Sy said.

"Or your sleeping bag," Chuck said. "Maybe you zip two sleeping bags together."

"Did you hear me, Chuck? Are you going to kill me? I don't believe you're going to—like I said before, I trust you—but if I'm wrong, if that's where this is headed, I'd like to know. If you don't hurt me—Chuck, I want you to hear me on this—if this thing stops here right now, it will stay just between you and me. I'll never tell anyone. Not even Vonda."

"Vonda is what is between you and me," Chuck said.

"I mean this, Chuck. I mean the whole thing with the gun here. This will stay just between you and me. This is what I won't tell anyone about. No one needs to know about this is all I'm saying."

"You can tell anyone you want," Chuck said, and he raised the pistol, pointed it and emptied the magazine.

Before the gunshots rang out, the men could hear chattering squirrels and scolding birds in the treetops, but afterward the woods were silent.

When Chuck lowered the pistol, the deer stand looked the same as it had before. The gun hadn't done any damage at all. It had made no difference.

Chuck grunted as he sidearmed the gun into the woods as far as he could throw it, and then he turned his back to Sy and took a few steps up the trail back toward the road. He didn't get very far, though, before pivoting to face Sy again.

"That was my father's pistol," Chuck said.

"I'm glad you didn't shoot me, Chuck," Sy said.

"World War II," Chuck said. "He just repaired trucks, but he got a gun. I regret flinging it away like that. I shouldn't have done that."

"We can probably find it without too much trouble," Sy said. "I think I saw about where it landed."

"I don't have any more bullets," Chuck said. "And I'm not going to get any more."

"I told you before that I trusted you," Sy said. "That's why I'm willing to help you."

The men moved through the brush toward where the gun landed. "The fire's opened up some holes back in here, so be careful," Sy said, and then he saw the gun almost immediately, and when Chuck's back was turned he picked it up, stuck it down the back of his pants, gradually made his way over to the rock bank, and slipped the gun into a large, smoking crevice. He didn't hear it hit bottom.

"I don't think I threw it quite that far," Chuck called over to Sy. "You're too far, I think. It's more like over this way."

Sy moved toward where Chuck was standing. "Hear me on this one thing, Chuck," Sy said. "Vonda never once said anything bad about you to me. You should know that. In a way, this didn't have anything to do with you. Does that sound harsh? I don't mean it to sound like that. I just mean what Vonda and I have is our own thing. I'm just trying to be straightforward here, Chuck. I know Vonda can speak for herself, and I know you two will have to hash things out. I just want you to know that I don't think what she and I have now is anyone's fault. Leastwise yours."

Chuck was hunched over, prying something from the ground. When he stood, he held a rusty pickaxe. The muddy ground was cool, but the handle felt warm in Chuck's hands.

"Hey, Sy," Chuck said. "Look at this, Sy. Look at what I found."

Gabe, 1995

Gabe follows the blood trail for what feels like a half-hour before finally catching sight of the buck. From a distance, it appears like it finally lay down to die in a clump of mushrooms, but when Gabe gets closer, he sees that, although he's right about its dying, what he thought were mushrooms on the mossy carpet of the woods' floor are actually tumors on the deer's body. The charcoal-gray growths look shiny and fragile, like bubbles. One patch spills from the buck's eye down into its mouth, and another thicker, larger mass covers the deer's flank, from shoulder to hindquarter. That's where Gabe shot him, where the buckshot and blood are. Just left of the tail. A deer in better shape maybe would've shaken it off and pulled through.

Gabe takes the walkie-talkie out of his jacket pocket and calls Jugger. "Found him."

"I was starting to wonder," Jugger answers. "How's he look?"

"Seven-pointer, but he's not a keeper."

"What do you mean?"

"You'll see. I wish I would've missed him altogether."

"All right. Well, where are you?"

"In the woods," Gabe says. "Under the sky."

"Come on," Jugger says. "I told you to pay attention when you were chasing him."

"There are trees all around me," Gabe says.

"Keep it up, and I'll leave you in the trees," Jugger says. "You can walk home in the trees."

"Take it easy," Gabe says. "I'm fine. I can see the highway from where I am."

"All right. How about I give myself another forty-five minutes or so to see what I can see, and then we can meet up on the road. I'll give you a shout when I leave."

"All right."

Gabe re-pockets the walkie-talkie, lays down his rifle and clears a spot for himself to sit down at the base of a large rock. He leans back and closes his eyes. It's been more than twenty-four hours, and he still feels full from yesterday's dinners. Two of them. He and Jeannette did the Thanksgiving tour. Noon at his parents' house, and then in the evening at Jeannette's grandmother's. Jeannette hardly ate anything, and he couldn't stop eating. "Well, I'm eating for two now, you know." He'd made the same joke at both places, and both times it had gotten a laugh. Not from Jeanette, though. When he delivered the line at his parents' house, she rolled her eyes, and later at her grandmother's house, she looked at him and shook her head as everyone else guffawed. Like he'd somehow disappointed her or let her down. He's not sure if it was the joke itself that bugged her or his repetition of the joke. Or maybe it wasn't the joke at all. Maybe she didn't like watching him make a pig of himself. Gabe slips a hand under his jacket and shirt and grabs his belly. Four months ago there'd been nothing there to grab. Since Jeannette told him about the baby, though, he hadn't run one mile or done one sit-up, and he'd started drinking beers at lunch with Jugger after Jugger got him on full-time at Weis's. Full benefits, too. Things couldn't have worked out better as far as that goes. Everyone told him as much, told him how fortunate he was that management had been willing to take him on, and everyone told Jeannette how fortunate she was to have someone like Gabe, someone who, even though he was so young, would step up like he did. He knew Jeannette didn't feel fortunate, though. He knew because he didn't feel fortunate either.

If Gabe were hunting with his father and his uncles, they already would have called the authorities about the sick deer. That's what you're supposed to do. Gabe's not sure what would happen after that. Maybe they'd be told to bring the deer somewhere or to stay with it until a Game Commission agent arrived. At any rate, Gabe knows Jugger won't want to do that. And he himself doesn't see the need for it. If another hunter comes along later and sees the carcass and wants to do things by the book, more power to him. Gabe told Jeannette he'd be home mid-afternoon, though, so he doesn't have time to dick around with the deer. He'd promised Jeannette they'd go see a movie tonight. He wants to see the new James Bond, and she wants to see *Toy Story* again, which probably means they'll see neither. They'll compromise instead. They'll see some other thing that neither of them is that into.

Gabe gets up and walks over to the deer. He grabs its legs and flips them over so he can get a look at the other side of its body, which is clean. Normal. The deer he thought he was shooting at.

Gabe wonders how the deer got sick. Probably tainted water. The streams and ditches around here smell like rotten eggs and get an orange tint to them after heavy rain and snow melt. Runoff from all the abandoned mines. Not to mention the fire and all the poison it's pumping out. It's a wonder all the deer don't look like this one. "Pretty soon the only thing left will be muskrats," he's heard his father and uncles say to each other. "A muskrat could thrive in a puddle of piss."

When Gabe drops the deer's legs and turns away again, a flash catches his eye. Up on the bank. When he gets there, he finds a metal flask wedged in a crack on the rock face. He kicks it free with his boot and picks it up, feels its warmth through his glove. He unscrews the cap and sniffs. Smoky sweet, like a burnt marshmallow.

A bit further up the bank, Gabe sees smoke drifting up from the rocks. Most of it seems to be coming from one large crevice, a bigger version of the smoke-belching seams that pock the fire-scarred highway. Driving down the stretch of closed road, Jugger had treated the potholes like they were part of an obstacle course. When Gabe told him in his ear to slow down, he instead sped up, and the four-wheeler screamed. A chorus of chainsaws.

Gabe pockets the flask, drops to all fours and starts climbing. Toward the crevice. To see what he can see.

NEW ROUTE 61

"What are we doing?" Lo says from the back seat. She's slumped, drowsy-eyed, open-bloused. The baby in her arms, Henry, is sleeping and nursing, sleeping and nursing.

"Pulling over," Webb says, easing the van off the highway. He turns off the engine and switches on the hazards. "We're not going any further until he's done. Back buckled up in his seat where he's supposed to be."

"He has to eat, he has to eat," Lo says, and she winces as she adjusts her son's head. "I told you twenty minutes back I wanted to stop. We could've pulled into Sheetz. I wanted a doughnut. I still want a doughnut."

"Well we're stopped here," Webb says, rolling his window halfway down. He reaches into the pocket of his hoodie for his pack of cigarettes and shakes one loose. "We don't need gas yet is why I didn't stop at Sheetz. Besides, is it a doughnut you want, or is it a chance to sneak a call to Ken?"

"No," Lo says. Her voice isn't angry or exasperated. It's matter-of-fact. "I told him everything I needed to tell him in the note I wrote. Nothing left to say. I'm done. For good this time. You'll see."

"I sure will see," Webb says. "Front row seat."

"You can't smoke when Henry's nursing," Lo says. "I have to tell you that?"

"Sorry," Webb says, rolling his window back up. "Sorry, Mommy. Sorry, Baby." He turns around in his seat and watches his nephew before looking up at Lo. "Looks like he's doing more snoozing than boozing," Webb says.

"He's been a lazy eater from day one," Lo says. She smoothes her son's hair and puts her mouth to his warm ear. "Lazy, lazy, lazy. Wake up, Lazy. Uncle Webb's getting impatient."

Webb shoves his cigarette in his lips and opens his door. "I'll be right out here."

"We'll be right in here," Lo says. "Right in here with no doughnuts." Webb watches the baby's hand crawl up his sister's cheek and find her mouth, watches Lo take the tiny hand in her own and kiss its fingers one at a time. Pinkie, ring, middle, fore, thumb.

Webb gets out of the van and closes the door behind him. He lights his cigarette and circles around back to check the U-Haul trailer. He's never before towed anything with the van, and he's nervous about everything staying hitched tight and together. In terms of the van's engine and transmission, he hopes he's not putting it through more than it can take. His father had bought it used when he started Rubinkam's Locksmith Services, Webb's business now, and Webb remembers his dad saying then that he'd be happy to get three or four years out of it. That was well over a decade ago. The van had outlasted Webb's father.

Webb sits on the van's rear bumper and tries to settle himself. He needs to get himself to believe Lo, and he needs to get himself to believe that Lo believes herself. That this time she's fully committed, that she's going to follow through. That this time she's finally had it with her cheating dirtbag of a husband. That no matter what Ken says, no matter what stunt he pulls to try to get her back, she won't let herself be gotten back. That once she and Henry are settled in Erie, she'll call a lawyer and file for divorce and get on with making a new life. Webb's talked himself into believing her a few times before, so he knows he has it in him. Just this one last time.

Webb thinks he feels a raindrop, and then another, but when he looks up he doubts himself. The horizon's clear, star-filled. Were it daytime, Webb wonders if he'd be able to see the smoke from the Centralia fire. When the fire worked its way under the highway, the road started to buckle and split, so they had to re-route 61. The turnoff for the old road's around here somewhere. In high school, Webb, Lo and their friends would drive out to it sometimes for parties. The state had blocked off the road with a mountain of dirt, so you had to park on the shoulder of the new highway, just like Webb and Lo are doing now, and then hoof it over the barrier to get out onto the old road. You weren't supposed to be there. That was part of the attraction. The spookiness, too. With the smoke rising from the potholes and the cracked blacktop, you knew you were somewhere cursed and dangerous. It was a great place to booze. They'd lug cans of spray paint with them, too. The road itself the canvas. Kids had been painting it for years, but if you hiked a ways you could still find blank sections. Lo was really good. Most of the kids, Webb included, would stick to letters and words—their initials or wise-ass comments about each other or punch-lines to inside jokes—but Lo painted actual pictures. The best one she did was of the devil. The idea behind it was that the old smoking road was the gateway to hell, and the devil was welcoming everyone home. Webb remembers some kid telling Lo that she should design T-shirts and posters or open a tattoo parlor. She was that good.

Webb studies the bright, unobscured moon, clipped to the front of the sky like a headlamp, and thinks of his dad, who, before starting the locksmith business, had worked in the mines for a while, up in Luzerne County. This was back when Lo and Webb were little kids, kindergarten-aged or even younger. When his father would get home from a shift, Webb can remember arguing with Lo over who'd get to wear his filthy helmet first and for how long. Whoever got to wear it would turn on the headlamp and shine it in the other's eyes, and this would cause a second argument. Webb remembers his mother settling the issue at least once by taking the helmet away, putting it on the high shelf in the mud room, telling them that it wasn't a toy.

Sometimes Webb thinks about how it may be best that his mom and dad are gone now. Tonight's one of those times. His parents had both died too young, but at least they'd been spared having to watch Lo go through these past few years with Ken. At least they'd missed all the pain and poison that came out of what once seemed to be normal, honest love. And being gone, they won't have to see Webb give up on the locksmith business. If that's what he ends up doing. All his friends are getting on with the fracking outfits and making money hand over fist, and Webb's close to joining them. He can make ends meet with the locksmithing, but that's about it. Nothing extra. If he got on a fracking crew, he could put some money away. He knows Lo and Henry are going to need some help for a while.

Lo's against it because of all the environmental stuff. When the well blew out in Clearfield, she cut out the story from the newspaper and saved it for him, and she showed him all the stories about aquifers and water wells getting contaminated and how Pennsylvania's the only state that allows companies to dump their waste frackwater straight into the rivers. Arsenic and lead and barium and strontium and chloride and trihalomethanes. Dimock and Beaver Falls and Hatfield Township. Webb sees a way to make some money, and suddenly Lo's a chemist and a protector of the motherland. "You sure you want to be part of an industry like that?" she says. "More harm than good. At least what you're doing now, you're helping people. You're not getting rich, but you're not making anyone sick."

Webb understands his sister's concerns, but he keeps telling her he isn't looking at the career change as a long-term thing. "Besides," he told her a few weeks ago, "I'd get the training through Penn State, at their Marcellus Shale Training Center, and Penn State also runs The Marcellus Shale

Research Center or whatever it is, so I'll be getting trained by the same institution that's studying the safety issues and pollution stuff." He thought he was making a good point, but she turned it around on him, wondered aloud if a center for training people to get jobs in an industry that was still being studied for its potential dangers and risks made any sense at all.

"So you're smarter than the professors and scientists in State College?" Webb said.

Instead of answering the question directly, Lo had taken another route. "Dad quit mining because of the danger and the environmental stuff, you know," she told Webb, "and now here you are wanting to do this craziness."

That's not how Webb sees it, though. And that's not how he remembers it. His dad told Webb he started his own business because he didn't want a boss any more. The thing about Lo is, in an argument, she'll say just about anything to win.

So on the one hand, with all that's going on, Webb's relieved in a way that his parents are gone, but on the other hand, he hates how they're missing out on being grandparents to Henry, and although it might be selfish, he can't help but think about how, if they were still around, the business of helping Lo wouldn't be solely and completely left to him. His parents would know better than he how to help their daughter. They'd know better about when and if to do more and when and if to do less.

Across the highway, a few hundred feet ahead, Webb watches a pickup stop in the middle of the road, idle for a few seconds, and then begin to back up and veer toward the shoulder. He can just make out two figures on the roadside moving forward to meet the truck, and when it stops, the two figures talk with the driver at the side window and then head around back to climb up and over the tailgate into the pickup's bed.

Webb watches the truck ease back onto the highway, but it doesn't get far. It slows as it approaches Webb, and when it draws even with him, it stops and idles again. Webb stands, flicks his cigarette into a clutch of roadside dandelions gone to seed, and waves at the truck. "We're OK," he calls out. "We're fine."

Webb's words are wasted, though. It's not until he's already done speaking that the pickup's passenger side window comes down.

"Everything all right?" The voice coming from the truck's dark window is female, old. "You need a phone? You need a tow?"

"We're fine, thanks," Webb says. "We're good."

"My son knows engines if you want him to take a look."

"No trouble," Webb says. "Just taking a break."

As Webb hears the old woman report his answer to the driver, he watches the hitchhikers in the bed stand and move toward the tailgate like they're looking to get out, like they've changed their minds about needing a ride after all. They move slowly and heavily, and Webb wonders if they're drunk or maybe disabled in some way.

The driver of the pickup doesn't realize his passengers are standing, doesn't realize they've changed their minds, so when he hears his help isn't needed, he puts the truck in drive and hits the gas. When the truck takes off, one of the hitchhikers loses his balance, stumbles toward the cab and into the other hitchhiker, and they both fall back into the bed. One of them caroms of the sidewall hard enough to knock whatever he was holding out of his hand, and whatever he was holding hits the highway with a clink and a spark and skids a few feet toward Webb.

As he watches the truck's taillights fade, Webb's heart flutters into his throat. He's thinking gun. The hitchhikers were probably looking to get out of the truck so they could do something to him. Rob him. Steal the van and all his tools, not to mention the U-Haul. Once they saw Lo and Henry in the back seat, who knows what might've gone down?

When Lo punches at her window with the side of her fist, Webb breathes deeply before opening the door and ducking his head in. "How we doing?" he says.

"Henry's done for now," Lo says. The baby's strapped in his car seat and playing with an empty pill bottle, shaking it for all he's worth. He wants it to make noise, but it won't. "We'll need to stop soon, though. Gas or no gas. Henry needs a diaper change, and I have to pee." She gestures down the road after the pickup. "What was that all about?"

"Just making sure we were OK."

"Good Samaritans," Lo says. "Did they have doughnuts? I bet you didn't even ask."

"We'll stop up ahead," Webb says. "There's a QuikMart in Catawissa. Just give me a sec."

Lo begins to say something back, but Webb shuts the door on it. He looks at her through the window then—her mouth's agape at his rudeness—and he raises his forefinger. "Hang on," he says. He turns toward the highway, checks for cars, and ventures out onto the blacktop.

The gun Webb's searching for turns out to be a flask. Webb smirks at himself as he bends down to pick it up, but curses and pulls back when it burns his fingers. Before reaching for it again, he pulls the sleeve of his sweatshirt over his hand like an oven mitt.

Shielding the flask with his body—he's not sure why, but he doesn't want Lo to see—he makes his way back to the rear bumper of the van. He holds the flask to his ear and shakes it. It feels and sounds empty, and when he unscrews the cap and tips it, just a few thin drops of liquid trickle out. Webb brings the flask to his nose. Smells like hot tar, like the stuff road crews use to fill potholes. He lets a warm drop settle onto his finger and brings it to the tip of his tongue. Tastes like smoky mud.

The flask is grimy and scorched black here and there, but it could be something worth cleaning up properly and keeping. Webb's not much of a drinker, but some things are just neat to have. When Webb realizes, though, that the top of the flask is dented, probably from the impact with the road, and that as a result the cap doesn't thread back on right, and the flask won't stop leaking even though it seems to be nearly empty, he decides it's more trouble than it's worth. So by the time Webb hears Lo's door open, his arm's already in motion, and by the time he hears Lo's voice—"Let's get going, Webb!"—the flask is already in the air, on its downward arc across the highway where it skips and tumbles over the bank and ultimately lands upright in a clump of purple deadnettle.

Forty-five minutes later, Lo and Henry wait in the Catawissa QuikMart as Webb plies his trade, curling himself under the steering wheel of a Ford Focus. The driver broke his key off in the ignition. The guy's passenger, his wife, has her set of keys—they're in the purse on her shoulder—but that fact isn't doing anyone any good because half the broken key is stuck in the lock cylinder.

The couple had expressed gratefulness and almost giddy surprise at their good fortune when Webb pulled up in the space next to them—"Rubinkam's Locksmith Services" painted in red block letters on both sides of his van—but just a few minutes into the job, the husband's tone is already shifting toward impatience and suspicion. Webb sees this all the time. Customers are happy when you show up, but at some point a switch flips, and they start getting antsy and ornery about time and cost.

"How long you think?" the guy asks. He's young, about Webb's age, but he's spiffed up, wearing a suit.

"Focuses can be tricky," Webb says. "You just want me to clear the cylinder, or do you want me to make you a new key, too?"

"Like we said, my wife has her key," the guy says. "I'll take care of that song and dance later."

"However you want to work it," Webb says.

"That's how," the guy says.

"Chill out, Andrew," the guy's wife says to him. She's sleeveless, hugging herself with goose-dimpled arms. "Don't get all worked up."

"If you're cold, honey, you should go on inside," the guy says to her. "Get yourself a coffee."

Webb stands, opens his kit and selects an extractor tool. "I'm usually pretty quick, but with a jammed ignition, if you go too fast or start forcing the issue, you can damage the tumblers. Your tumblers get damaged, you're stuck taking the car into the shop for a whole new ignition."

"So take your time then," the guy says. "I was just wondering how long."

It's just as the guy finishes saying this that the busted key comes sliding out of the cylinder like a dream, and Webb feels a lot of satisfaction in dropping it in the guy's palm. This satisfaction, though, is short-lived. As Webb starts to put the car's steering column back together, he realizes he's short a set screw. Twenty minutes later, he and the couple are still looking for it. The husband, cursing under his breath now, heads into the store to see if he can buy a flashlight because the one that Webb keeps in his van isn't working no matter how hard or how many times Webb slaps it or bangs it against his knee.

As Webb continues to scour the inside of the car—his search has led him over the center console to the passenger seat, his thinking being that the screw might have bounced or sprouted wings and flew—the wife leans into the car to ask Webb a question. Might the screw be on him somewhere? Maybe up his sleeve or down the front of his sweatshirt? "When I lose a contact lens, that's usually where I find it," the woman says. "On myself."

The woman's breath is stinky sweet. Alcohol and breath mints. Could be her breath smells like this a lot, or it could be tonight's a special occasion. At any rate, Webb likes it. At Lo and Ken's wedding reception, Webb had a couple slow dances with one of Ken's cousins, and her breath smelled like this, too.

As Webb stands to take the woman's advice and pat himself down, he wonders if maybe the flask he'd found back on Route 61 might not have been a bad thing to keep after all. He should've thrown it in the back of the van and decided later whether it was worth the effort or not. If it had turned out to be restorable, Webb could see himself bringing the flask with him on a visit to Erie sometime down the road, maybe six months or a year from now when things seem settled. At night, after Henry's tucked in, Webb can imagine surprising his sister with the flask—whistle-clean, polished, and filled with Southern Comfort, Lo's favorite—and he can imagine the two of them proceeding to toast cut ties and new beginnings. At some point, of course, Webb would tell Lo when and where the flask had come from. He'd tell her about the hitchhikers and how he'd thought they were coming for him, how he'd thought the flask was a gun. This was just after he'd almost smoked in the car even though Henry was nursing and just after he'd had himself convinced it was raining even though the moon was out, shining like the headlamp on Dad's old miner's helmet.

"I was wrong about everything that night," he can imagine himself saying, and he'd consider telling her how, while working on that jammed ignition in the parking lot, he'd worried she was in the QuikMart's ladies room, huddled with Henry in a stall, crying into the phone at Ken and listening to him cry back at her. He shouldn't let himself tell her this, though. It would ruin the mood. Instead, he'll confess something else, something less crucial.

That Focus he'd worked on? That steering column set screw he'd lost? "You know where I ended up finding it? Pocket of my sweatshirt. My own pocket." Webb imagines Lo laughing and then shushing herself because Henry's sleeping down the hall and then laughing again anyway. Webb imagines himself laughing, too. And he imagines having an envelope for her. An envelope with a check in it, a check big enough to choke her up. Or not. He doesn't have an envelope for her, but the van is parked outside at the curb, and she's happier about that than she would have been about an envelope. Either way. They'd be happy either way. At how things had turned out all right despite all the mistakes and screw-ups. Despite all the things about which Webb had been dead wrong.

AUTUMN HOUSE FICTION SERIES

New World Order • Derek Green

■ *Drift and Swerve* • Samuel Ligon

Monongahela Dusk • John Hoerr

■ *Attention Please Now* • Matthew Pitt

■ *Peter Never Came* • Ashley Cowger

Keeping the Wolves at Bay: Stories by Emerging American Writers • Sharon Dilworth, ed.

Party Girls • Diane Goodman

■ *Favorite Monster* • Sharma Shields

New America: Contemporary Literature for a Changing Society • Holly Messitt and James Tolan, eds.

Little Raw Souls • Steven Schwartz

■ *What You Are Now Enjoying* • Sarah Gerkensmeyer

■ *Come by Here* • Tom Noyes

■ Winner of the Autumn House Fiction Prize

DESIGN AND PRODUCTION

Cover and text design by Kathy Boykowycz

Text set in Minion, designed by Robert Slimbach in 1990

Printed by McNaughton and Gunn on Glatfelter Natural Offset, an FSC certified paper